The Stablemaster's Daughter

BARBARA DEVLIN

DEDICATION

This book is for all the stablemasters' daughters of the world. Never let anyone tell you that you don't belong..

NOTE FROM BARBARA DEVLIN

This book contains descriptions of child abuse, and it is important that the reader know I did not treat the very serious theme gratuitously. Rather, my goal is to reassure anyone who's ever suffered such abuse that there is life after the pain. I know this, because I am a survivor of physical abuse, I am Ernest, and much like the character I've created, the abuse is a secret I've long kept until now. You see, I am the product of a broken home, and for whatever reason my mother took out her anger with my father against me. The child in me never understood why she hurt me, but the adult in me knows I didn't deserve what happened to me. However, the abuse impacted who I am, and I'm working to change that, after all these years. This note is the first step in that direction. I've kept secrets all my life. I still keep secrets—I excel at it. I hide myself from the world, afraid to share even the most joyous achievements, because I'm so accustomed to living in the shadows. To hiding. I suffer anxiety when bringing attention to myself, because I've always avoided the spotlight, which often brought more abuse. If you're like me, if you've been beaten for simply existing, know you're not alone, and you didn't deserve to be hurt. You deserve to be loved.

~Barb

PROLOGUE

London
October 11, 1812

A shrill scream reverberated through the house, piercing the quiet, and Lord Ernest Cornelius Frederick Howe bolted upright in bed. Rubbing his eyes, he yawned and wondered if he dreamed the blood-curdling shriek, until another hair-raising shout of alarm had him leaping from bed.

After pulling on his wool breeches, he donned his silk robe, belted it at the waist, and sprinted, bare-footed, into the hall. A small army of servants ran down the corridor, toward his elder brother's suite. Curious, Ernest followed suit.

At the double-door entry to the marquess's private apartment, the butler loomed, with a grim expression. "My lord, something terrible has happened."

"What is it?" Myriad thoughts echoed in his brain, and Ernest swallowed hard. "Is it Barrington?"

"No, sir." Ashby shook his head. "It is one of the maids."

"What about her?" Ernest pushed past the butler, crossed the sitting room, and rushed into the bedchamber, where Doolittle, Barrington's valet, averted his gaze and compressed his lips. It was then Ernest glanced at the massive four-poster, and he almost retched. "Oh, my god."

Violent crime was the curse of the poor, not the elite of society, and never had he witnessed anything so brutal. Blood trailed from one side of the mattress to the other, with large crimson spatters dotting the once pristine white sheets.

Lying face up, nude, and prostrate, one of the housemaids, whose name he could not recall in the shock of the moment, had been stabbed to death in Barrington's bed. Her lifeless eyes fixed on the elegant canopy, with her mouth agape in a silent scream, and never would he forget the morbid sight.

"Ashby, gather the household staff at the servant's dining table, and send a footman to

Bow Street, for the Runners." The butler nodded and rushed into the hall. To Doolittle, Ernest asked, "Where is my brother?"

"To my knowledge, His Lordship never came home last night." The valet scratched the back of his neck and shifted his weight, as though he was agitated, and that gave Ernest pause. "Often Lord Ravenwood stays out, but it is not my place to inquire after his plans."

Reflecting on the situation, Ernest could glean no rhyme or reason to the senseless act, and Barrington had no mistress. In fact, he never entertained courtesans, because it was no secret the elder Howe loved his fiancée, Lady Florence Wilfred.

Ernest loved someone, once. But that was long ago, and he knew not what became of her, after she was taken from him, when they were but children. He often thought of searching for her, but he never did, because he feared what he might find. That she might have found happiness without him.

But that was not the issue, at the moment, and he snapped into action.

So where was his brother?

"Take the back stairs and wait for His Lordship in the mews." Ernest lowered his voice. "Tell him what happened, so he is not surprised when he returns to find the authorities in our home. I would not have him caught unaware."

"Aye, sir." Doolittle dipped his chin and exited the apartment.

A final glance at the horrific scene revealed a knife near the base of the footboard. Peering over his shoulder, Ernest checked to ensure no one witnessed his questionable behavior, as he pulled a handkerchief from the tallboy, squatted, wrapped the bloody weapon in the square of linen, and slipped it into his robe pocket.

No, it was not the honorable thing to do, but it was the right thing for the situation, and he wagered he would pay for it, later.

Retreating into the sitting room, Ernest drew shut the double doors and flagged a footman. "Stand guard until the Runners arrive, and permit no one entry."

"Aye, my lord," the servant replied.

Calm and collected, Ernest strolled back to his chamber, drew forth the knife, and studied the crude but lethal armament. Not for a minute did he suspect Barrington committed the murder, but Ernest would take no chances with his brother's liberty and his family's social standing, so he hid the dagger in his armoire.

At the washstand, he splashed water on his face and cleaned his teeth. His heart weighed heavy in his chest, as he dressed in a crisp white shirt, sans cravat, a dark blue hacking jacket, and polished Hessians. In the long mirror, he scrutinized his appearance and ran his fingers through his blond hair.

"I am doing the right thing." At least, if he told himself that enough, he just might believe it. Yet it seemed some things never changed, because Ernest had spent a lifetime picking up after his older brother, when their relationship should have operated in the reverse. "But Barrington had better have a damn good explanation."

With that, he inhaled a deep breath, turned on a heel, and trod into the storm he prayed was not of his sibling's making. On the landing, two gentlemen conversed with the butler, and Ernest rolled his shoulders when they noted his approach.

"My lord." Ashby stepped aside. "These men are from Bow Street." He pointed to a tall, swarthy looking character. "This is Inspector Kenworth, of the Runners."

"Lord Ernest, it is a pleasure to make your acquaintance, under such inauspicious circumstances." Kenworth half-bowed.

"And may I introduce Special Agent Miles Barrett, of the Counterintelligence Corps. In cases involving members of the peerage, the Home Office requires we notify the corps."

"Lord Ernest." A shrewd but elegantly dressed character, Agent Barrett nodded once. "Your butler explained some of the circumstances surrounding the murder."

"Thank you for coming so quickly." Ernest extended a hand in welcome. "Permit me to show you the body."

"Can you provide a list of those who entered the scene?" Agent Barrett brushed past the footman and scrutinized the entrance. "And who discovered the deceased?"

"My brother's valet, Duncan Doolittle." Ernest led the investigators through the sitting room, to the inner chamber. "But before he could warn Ashby, a maid happened upon the body and shouted the alarm."

"I will need to interview everyone, beginning with Lord Ravenwood." Inspector Kenworth paused at the foot of the bed. "Do you know the victim?"

"Yes." Ernest swallowed hard, as he glanced at the youthful face bereft of her customary animated smile. "Her name is Ellen, and Ashby can provide additional information regarding her background, as she has been in our employ for a few years. And my brother is not in residence."

"Where is Lord Ravenwood?" Inspector Kenworth inquired.

"I am not sure." Ernest shuffled his feet. "It does not appear he slept at home, last night."

"Can you vouch for him?" Agent Barrett narrowed his stare. "And what of your whereabouts?"

"I was in my bed." It was then Ernest realized they viewed him as a suspect, and he was not prepared for that. "But no one can provide proof of what I say, because I slept alone." Shuffling his feet, he tried to ignore his racing pulse. "As for my brother, I have no direct knowledge of his current location or intimate habits, as I am not his keeper, and he does not share that information with me. But, to my knowledge, he has not been home."

And the family could ill afford a scandal, given the tenuous state of the marquessate's finances, and his father always insisted that blood relations reigned supreme, above all else. It was something he beat into his younger son, with cruel regularity, so Ernest would do everything in his power to protect Barrington.

"When was the last time you spoke with

him?" Using a bull's-eye lantern, Kenworth scrutinized the carpets, and Ernest pondered the bloody knife hidden in his chamber. Had he missed something of significance? "And did he behave in a suspicious manner?"

"I am not sure what you mean, because I do not believe, for an instant, that Barrington killed that poor woman." Ernest checked his tone. "And I took a brandy with him, yesterday evening, at White's." He searched his memory to recall the specifics. "It was about five-thirty, and the rooms were crowded, so there are plenty of witnesses who could support my account."

"We will verify that for the official record, Lord Ernest." Agent Barrett squatted near the footboard and appraised a bloodstain on the counterpane. "It is just routine, and we mean no insult."

"Investigative teams should arrive, soon, to commence a sweep for clues and evidence." Inspector Kenworth stood upright and adjusted his coat. "Until then, we should seal the apartment."

"Of course." Ernest led them to the hall, where he signaled the footman. "Permit no one entry without the expressed permission of Inspector Kenworth or Agent Barrett."

"Aye, sir." The footman nodded and

resumed his guard.

Just then, the valet appeared, and Ernest stiffened his spine. "Please, excuse me." He waved, and Doolittle strolled toward the gallery. Lingering near a bust of the third marquess of Ravenwood, Ernest folded his arms. "What is it?"

"His Lordship returned, and he hides in your quarters." Doolittle opened his mouth and then closed it. "He is innocent, sir. He did not sleep in residence."

"I know that." Ernest peered over his shoulder. "Stay here, and say nothing to the authorities."

"Yes, my lord." Doolittle clasped his hands before him. "And I remain loyal to Lord Ravenwood, as always."

"I know that, too." And it did not surprise Ernest, because everyone loved Barrington. Indeed, he was the golden child.

Whereas Ernest was the second son, the lesser Howe.

In mere minutes, Ernest crossed the landing and navigated the corridor to his private accommodation. Careful not to draw attention to himself, he turned the knob, pushed open the oak panel, and slipped into his sitting room, but it was empty.

"*Psst.*" In the bedchamber, Barrington

partially hid behind a drapery panel and waved. "In here."

"Brother, what are you doing?" Ernest frowned as they locked forearms. "There is a Runner and an agent from the Counterintelligence Corps in the house, and you are not safe."

"So Doolittle told me, but I killed no one, as I was not in residence last night." With a wild-eyed gaze, Barrington glanced about, as if anticipating an assault. "What should I do, when I am the lone suspect in a crime I did not commit? And who would do such a thing? Who would conspire to entrap me?"

"I know not, but now is not the time to discuss it. Go to my bachelor's lodging, and wait for me, there." Ernest considered the knife but did not mention it. "Together, we can sort out this mess and plan a response. Then, we shall summon our solicitor, to protect your interests."

"Not a chance." Barrington scoffed. "I am leaving England, at once."

"What?" Gritting his teeth, Ernest summoned patience. "If you have done nothing wrong, if you have nothing to hide, why would you flee? Do you not see how it will appear?" He canted his head. "Where were you? Who were you with? All you need do is provide support for an alibi, as well as a witness to that effect, and you will be cleared."

"What if I cannot do that?" Barrington averted his stare. "They will give me a fair trial, and hang me. I must run, else I am doomed."

"Brother, no."

With that, Barrington broke free and ran into the sitting room, with Ernest following closely.

"I must leave, now."

"Where are you going?" He caught his brother by the elbow, but Barrington wrenched loose. "When do you suppose you will return, and what should I tell the authorities?" Without a response, the elder Howe opened the door and tiptoed into the hall. "Barrington—*come back*."

Alone. More alone than he had ever been in his life, Ernest just stood there and blinked. At last, he shook himself alert, retraced his steps, looked out the window, and sighed.

Some things never changed.

CHAPTER ONE

Derbyshire
January, 1819

It was a universally accepted principle that no good deed ever went unpunished. For Ernest, love of scandal manifested an inherent flaw of the human race, which often encouraged society to kick a man when he was low, and he endured almost five years of such abuse, in a particularly extended campaign that tested the limits of his patience, given he did nothing wrong. Indeed, in light of the outcome in the wake of the scandal that rocked his family, he did everything right, yet he remained an outcast.

As the second son in an estimable lineage, he worked hard to fulfill the expectations of those who should not matter but whose criticism he tried but failed to ignore. So he endeavored to persevere in a world governed by shallow appearances and easy friendships, which often altered with the wind, that he might persist not so much in happiness, because that was not possible without the woman he loved, but in a constant state of ennui.

How often he thought of his little bird, Henrietta. But her father sent her to live in Kent, eleven years ago, and he had no word from her, despite the letters he dispatched. At some point, he simply stopped writing, yet he never forgot her, and he hoped she was happy.

"Why so quiet, brother?" Barrington, the eldest Howe and the marquess of Ravenwood, drew rein, as they toured the eastern border of the estate that surrounded the ancestral pile, Garring Manor. "I had hoped we could talk, as you have scarcely uttered a word, since you arrived from London."

"I am not sure what you want me to say." The pain of the past unfurled and flared, blanketing him in a morbid chill, and Ernest swore under his breath, at the unfairness of it all. "You fled an accusation of murder, abandoned the marquessate and your fiancée, took up piracy, committed untold heinous offenses during five years on the run, which necessitated an official pardon from the Crown, and yet you are summarily forgiven and embraced by the *ton*." He snorted. "On the other hand, I stayed and fought the good fight. In your absence, I defended you, I settled our debts, sparing us an embarrassing declaration of insolvency, and I did my best to protect Lady Florence, yet I remain a social pariah."

"That is because people adore a scandal and a villain, second only to a tale of salvation and love, which I gave them." Barrington shrugged. "While it is not fair, I would argue there are few things in life that are just. For most, I represent the ultimate redemption story, because the devotion of a good woman helped me see the err of my ways, I returned to London, faced my demons, married a lady, got her with child, and all is forgiven." He glanced left and right, waggled his brows, and then he leaned near. "What most do not realize is that in the bedchamber, I remain very much a buccaneer."

"I am so happy for you." Ernest rolled his eyes, because, as usual, Barrington reduced everything to matters of the flesh. "So what do you suggest I do, take a wife and start a family, just to appease the horde?" The mere thought sent a shiver of dread down his spine, because his heart belonged to another. "Any candidate, in mind?"

"That is for you to decide, as I found my mate, but you must admit the idea holds merit, and you never know what tomorrow may bring." Barrington shifted in the saddle. "For what do you wait, as you are not getting any younger? And you have a natural instinct for cultivating relationships, as evidenced by your ability to thoroughly assume my position without the rank, while I was away."

"And we travel full circle." Frustrated, Ernest gritted his teeth. "Why must you throw that in my face, when you know my motives were honorable?"

"Ah, but you mistake my meaning." Chuckling, which only unnerved Ernest more; Barrington stuck his tongue in his cheek. "You see, had I attempted something so brazen, I would have failed miserably, because I have not your talent with words. But without the proper credentials, you secured the requisite credit to maintain Garring Manor and Howe House. Then you convinced a reputable barrister to take a case no one expected you to win, and you lost only because you could produce no proof of my demise. And had my stubborn bride not enacted a pretend illness to avoid the altar, you might have married her."

"In hindsight, I am grateful she persisted, because you own her heart—you always have." And Ernest did not love Florence, at least, not like that. He considered her more a sister than anything else. "And I only wanted to safeguard her, given the horrid gossip that plagued her, after you left. You know how the *ton* can be with scandalous figures."

"I know that, now." His elder sibling frowned. "But when I was alone, my thoughts conjured the most awful conclusions, and I regret that."

"I can accept that." Ernest focused on the horizon, as the agony resurfaced and swelled. Indeed, the anguish cut to the core. "What I will never understand is how you could have suspected me of committing the murder of one of our maids and attempting to cast blame on you for the barbarous offense, when I did naught but defend you. That is what hurts, brother. That is what functions as a very real barrier between us, given you know not what I sacrificed to protect you, unwittingly against our aunt and the butler with whom she conspired to steal the marquessate for our unfortunate and unworldly cousin who never aspired to such lofty heights. I never doubted your innocence, and you thought the worst of me, and that brings me so very low."

"And I would make amends, but I ask that you not judge me too harshly, as I never would have guessed Aunt Esther was capable of collaborating with Ashby to perpetrate such an awful deed, which also involved killing you, just to claim my title. Indeed, you were in as much danger as I, thus we should be allies. Yet, the negative effects of her offense lingers, and she wreaks further havoc, as you and I remain at odds, and I would put to rest the past, if you let me." Barrington made it sound so simple to atone for old injuries, and that was his downfall. Born into power and privilege, everything came easy to him, whereas Ernest, the second son, worked for his fortune. And their father had an unusual method for inspiring Ernest. "Tell me what to do, and I shall do it."

"Therein lies the rub." He trailed the flight of a graceful osprey, as it soared through the sky. "Some things cannot be effortlessly erased. They endure. They fester. They poison all successive connections, rendering the afflicted a forsaken soul, to wander through life in misery and solitude."

"No." Barrington shook his head. "I will not allow that to happen to us. Yes, I made mistakes, but I learned that nothing is set in stone, and you and I are no different. We will retrench, brother. I swear on my firstborn, we will recover."

Of course, Barrington thought Ernest referenced his brother.

It never occurred to anyone that he missed Henrietta. That she, alone, occupied his thoughts, to the detriment of all else.

"I wish I shared your optimism." But from Ernest's perspective, the future appeared rather bleak, given his lack of prospects. "If you do not mind, I would prefer to tour the north fields on my own, as I need to think."

"As you wish." With that, Barrington saluted and turned his stallion. "Then I believe I will join Florence for a nap, because she rests better with me at her side. When you are ready to resume our discussion, I am at your disposal."

Heeling the flanks of his hunter, Ernest steered toward the dirt path that led to the most picturesque part of their ancestral estate in the Peak District. As he charged the verge, the resplendent vista of a clear azure sky, amid which a peregrine danced in search of prey, and vibrant verdure spread before him. It was a place in which he always found comfort, as he reminisced of cherished childhood memories and simpler times. Indeed, it was the only point in his life he was happy.

As he bent to clear a decumbent branch, a swatch of bright color caught his gaze, amid the canopy of a massive yew, and he noted a shapely calf. "Oy. Is someone there?"

A feminine shriek portended doom, and he urged his mount forward, just as a tangle of ruffles and lace dropped into his lap. Given the damsel in distress landed facedown, he admired her shapely bottom, as the skirt of her sprigged muslin dress stretched taut across her derriere.

"Oh, dear." She shifted in his grasp, yanked on her wool pelisse, and her elbow bumped his most prized protuberance, which woke with a vengeance. "My, but you gave me such a fright, and you really should not have shouted like that. Are you all right?"

"You fell from a tree, almost breaking your lovely neck, and you worry about me?" As he flipped her over and upright, he glimpsed the most astonishing, velvety brown eyes, which seemed to see right through him. For a moment, she stared at him, and he admired her heart-shaped profile, her pert little nose, her lush red lips, and her thick chestnut locks, which struck him as oddly familiar. Indeed, there was something comforting in her expression, as if he knew her, yet that was not possible. "Are you sure you are not injured?"

"Hello." Favoring him with a welcoming smile, she stunned him, when she wrapped her arms about his shoulders and hugged him. "How are you?"

"Much better, now." As she pressed her soft and feminine body to his, he savored her warmth and tried to calm the fully loaded cannon in his crotch, because it had been more than two months since he parted ways with his last importuning mistress, and the beast was hungry. "Are you always so friendly to strangers?"

~

"Strangers?" Henrietta Katherine Graham studied the man who had occupied her thoughts and dreams for the better portion of her life, especially the last eleven years, and blinked in astonishment, because she could never forget him. Yet, it was painfully clear Ernest did not recognize her.

How many nights had she planned their reunion? Too many to count. But in her fantasy, he welcomed her, as would an old, treasured friend. Quick as a wink, she recovered her wits, tamped her dismay, and rallied. "Why, I presumed you knew all the ladies in these parts, or are you not Lord Ernest Howe?"

"So did I." He chuckled in his signature tenor, which harkened to honey on a hot scone. "And you are correct." Tightening his hold, he canted his head and grinned. "May I escort you somewhere, Miss—"

"Actually, I planned to tour the north fields, as I cherish many fond memories there." When he arched a brow and his muscles tensed beneath her, betraying his not so indifferent state, she smiled, as she would claim that small victory. "Since you journey the same path, perhaps you will consent to join me?"

"You know my ancestral estate?" He nudged the impressive hunter, and they traveled further into the grove of trees, as she studied the lines about his eyes. "Let me guess. You are Lord Clifton's daughter, and you venture, unescorted, into the countryside to rebel against your father's overbearing manner."

"I know Garring Manor quite well." In play, she averted her stare, cursing his assumption, but she should have known he would think her a lady, as he was always a proper sort. "And I know no such connection, although my motives may prove just as bold."

"But you know my family?" In so many ways, he had not changed a bit. His once unruly, wavy blond hair had been close-cropped, yet it framed his chiseled patrician features, and his eyes, so crisp and clear, cut to her core. It was the remarkable transformation of his physique, especially his broad shoulders and strong arms, which set her heart racing, as he embraced her in his lap, and she could sit there for hours, as she did when they were children. "You are acquainted with my brother, Barrington?"

"In some respects, I know your family as well as my own." Henrietta nodded, still disappointed that he did not recognize her. "And I am very familiar with Lord Ravenwood, as well as his wife, Lady Florence."

"Then you must give me a hint." As they emerged from the copse of ancient yews, beneath which they once sat and ate sweetmeats he pilfered from his mother's fancy tea parties, Ernest anchored an arm about her waist, heeled the flanks of his horse, and set a blazing pace across a picturesque meadow, and she could not contain a squeal of delight. "Please, I beg you, as the anticipation is killing me. What is your name?"

"Oh, no." Resting her head to his chest, she giggled, as she teased him, just like old times. "This is too much fun."

"So you are a temptress." With that, he flicked the reins, and they soared down a hill, laughing all the way. "Do you know what becomes of such women?"

"I cannot imagine, sir." Nestled in his embrace, Henrietta rode a wave of unshakeable confidence. "Do tell."

Slowing to a halt, he cupped her chin. "They are destined to be ravished by their pursuer."

"And that is bad?" In truth, she would not protest being ravished by her childhood sweetheart, because he held her heart. He always had. Given the intensity of his scrutiny, she swallowed hard, as he focused his attention on her mouth. If only he would kiss her. Then he would recall that special day, beneath the yew on Oker Hill, when they first touched lip to lip. To her surprise, he bent his head and inched near. In a whispery summons, she beckoned, "*Ernest.*"

Dismay functioned as a bitter pill, when he flinched, retreated, and cleared his throat. "I should return to Garring Manor."

"Time for high tea?" As usual, she concealed her chagrin behind a polite façade born of years of practice, in service to the noble classes.

"Indeed." With the skill of a master equestrian, he turned the hunter. "Would you be my guest for an afternoon refreshment?"

"What a marvelous suggestion." And just like that, her spirits lifted. "Do you still favor the souchong?"

"How do you know my preference?" He frowned and then snapped his fingers. "Are you one of the Beauchamp girls?"

"Fie on you, sir." Now that insult stung, because they were nasty termagants. "Which of those two braying asses do you imply I resemble?"

"*Ha.*" In a moment of levity, he settled a palm to her hip, in a brazen display of intimacy. Then he started, as if she burned him. "Forgive me, as I took liberties."

"Believe me, Lord Ernest, it is not the first time." To ease the tension, Henrietta elbowed him. "And I hope it will not be the last."

"Upon my word, but you are a saucy lady." Soon, he would discover she was no lady, as they passed the main gate. "Please, I beg you, tell me your name."

When she shook her head, he groaned.

At the grand entry of the Portland stone mansion, which she once looked upon as her home, Henrietta slipped from his grasp and gained her footing. A stablehand held the lead, as Ernest dismounted. Arm in arm, they crossed the threshold of the elegant structure, and she marveled at how little changed from what she recalled.

From the gold flocked wall coverings and mahogany paneling and trim, to the Aubusson carpets and the James Reynolds long case clock, with its ebony trim and shallow champfer top surmounted by a gilt urn finial, the house seemed frozen in time, and she glanced at her appearance in the oval hall mirror. After tucking a stray tendril behind her ear, she smoothed her skirts and faced her host.

"Brother?" In the side hall, Lord Ravenwood, sans coat and cravat, strolled forth, carrying a tray, with a couple of covered dishes, a teapot, cups, and saucers. "I thought you were for an extended ride."

"I was, until an unexpected visitor landed in my lap." Ernest tugged the bell pull. "Were you not supposed to nap with Florence?"

"That was the plan, but she is hungry." It

was then Barrington noted her presence, and he smiled. "Hello, Henrietta. Your father told me of your impending visit, which I withheld from Ernest, because I thought it best to let you surprise my brother, and I see you did. When did you arrive?"

"*Hen*?" Ernest's eyes widened, evoking her nickname.

"Yesterday." She gulped. "Late in the evening, to be exact."

"My sincerest sympathies, over the loss of your aunt." Barrington strolled to the grand staircase. "How was your journey from Kent?"

"*Hen*?" Ernest rested fists on hips.

"Thank you, Lord Ravenwood." She shifted her weight and wrung her fingers. "And it was a long drive, so I was happy to reach my destination."

"Your father has spoken of nothing else." Barrington chuckled. "And Florence was thrilled, as she increases with our second child."

"*Hen*?" Ernest seemed on the verge of an apoplectic fit.

Finally, Barrington exhaled and said to Ernest, "Why do you keep repeating her name?"

"Because he did not recognize me." And

she hated to admit it.

"You must be joking." Barrington scoffed. "Though I must say you have grown since we last met. What were you, eleven? Twelve?"

"She was eight." Ernest's expression softened, and his cheeks boasted a charming shade of pink, as he took her hands in his. Was it her imagination, or did tears well in his eyes? "And I was but twelve."

"Then I shall leave you to your happy reunion." Barrington turned and ascended the stairs. Halfway up, he halted. "It is good to have you home, dear friend. You have been too long from Garring."

"Thank you." For a few minutes, she held Ernest's stare, and so many emotions invested his countenance.

"You rang, sir?" A very proper butler bowed.

"Ah, there you are, Crawford." Ernest tucked her at his side. "Miss Graham and I will take tea, scones, and some strawberry preserves, in the back parlor."

So he remembered her partialities.

"Yes, my lord." Crawford nodded once.

Again, silence fell on the foyer, and she wondered if she should have stayed in Kent.

At last, Ernest dragged Henrietta down the narrow corridor, to the rear of the grand

residence.   In   the   lush   appointed   but
comfortable gathering place, he hauled her to
the   center   of   the   room,   pulled   her   into   his
arms, and kissed her.

CHAPTER TWO

The sun rose on the horizon, on a brisk morning, as Ernest, of singular purpose, skipped down the back stairs. On the ground floor, he paused to assess his appearance, brushed a speck of lint from his navy-blue hacking jacket, adjusted his cravat, and smoothed his hair, because he wanted to look perfect. Nervous, though he could not say why, he paced for a few minutes, swore under his breath, and turned on a heel. After exiting the house via the terrace doors, he cut across the rose garden and traversed the graveled path that led to the stables. The seemingly simple practice was once part of his everyday routine, yet he had not traveled that walkway in eleven years.

In the yard, he signaled a hand. "Prepare two horses. My stallion and the sweet-tempered chestnut mare, which will require a sidesaddle."

"Aye, my lord." The stablehand nodded.

To the right of the carriage house sat a charming cottage, in which the stablemaster lived, and it had been his home away from home, once. It had been Ernest's sanctuary. After Hen departed Garring, the modest abode functioned as a painful reminder of his loss, so he avoided the place. Rolling his shoulders, he knocked on the door and folded his arms.

As anticipated, Graham set wide the heavy wood panel. "My lord, am I remiss in my duties?" He glanced toward the stables. "Are the hands not at their posts, or is there something you require of me, personally?"

"Everything is fine, Graham." Ernest unfolded his arms. "I came to ask Hen to accompany me on a ride."

"Of course, my lord." Casting a deep-set frown, the stablemaster stepped aside. "When last I checked, she was washing dishes and tidying the kitchen. Will you come inside, while I fetch her?"

"Thank you." The humble but clean accommodation harkened to so many happy reveries, as Ernest revisited his personal history and countless hours spent in play.

There, he was naught more than a lad of no account, with no expectations or responsibilities. He was simply Ernest. And so much of his childhood revolved around Henrietta, his little bird, and she was mistaken in her assertion, because he never forgot her.

Rather, he tucked her in that special part of his memory reserved for the most meaningful moments of his life.

Isolated from the harsh realities of his less-than-charmed existence, she could remain whole and pure, a balm to provide comfort and succor during his darkest days, and of those there had been many since they parted. Often, he summoned her, envisioning her as some benevolent angel swooping in to save him, and in his reveries she never disappointed him.

What he had not anticipated was the remarkable transformation of the girl to the irresistible woman. In so many ways, she presented a blank canvas. She was the ingénue. The provincial. The delicate flower just waiting to be plucked, and normally he looked past such frivolities, because his tastes ran toward the more seasoned ladies, when it came to his mistresses.

But when it came to Hen, his thoughts turned in a decidedly different direction, despite their long separation, and it was his body that all but screamed his choice. Because in all their years apart, no woman had commanded his senses as had Hen, and he could not ignore his reaction to her, when he knew not her true identity. Indeed, it was as though their estrangement had never happened. As a lad, he had been attracted to her. As a man, he had to have her.

"Good morning, Ernest." Pretty as a picture, with her brown locks artfully arranged in a pile of curls, and a frock of impeccable design, she could have passed for a noblewoman, if not for the apron. Still, such pedestrian accessories did not deter him from his goal. "Papa said you wished to see me."

"I had thought we might tour the ancient yews, as we did when we were young." He doffed his hat and cleared his throat. "That is to say, it would be my honor if you would accompany me."

To his delight, she squealed, clapped her hands, bounced with unveiled enthusiasm, turned on a heel, hiked her skirts, and ran down the hall, as she peered over her shoulder and shouted, "Give me five minutes to change into my habit."

The stress of his adult responsibilities seemed to melt in the face of her uninhibited spirit, reminding him of his younger, bolder self, because never had he inspired such a strong reaction in a woman beyond the confines of his bed. In her glowing gaze, Ernest spied the ardor of an untroubled soul and recalled a time when he, too, enjoyed an unfettered existence. His heart raced, and a renewed zest for adventure charged his nerves.

Once, in a place that seemed naught more than a fantasy, he expected he would marry Hen. Would build a life with her. Would create a family with her. Would spend his days endeavoring to keep the smile on her delicate countenance. Would grow old, together. Yet all those fanciful dreams changed in the blink of an eye, and he knew not why or how it came to pass.

As if by some cruel twist of fate, he transported back to that portentous afternoon, when he ventured to that very spot and found her gone. Her father's words echoed in Ernest's ears, the emptiness, the agony wrenched his insides, and he wiped his brow. Innocence died in that moment, and he cried himself to sleep for weeks, afterward, until his sire shuffled Ernest off to Eton.

"My lord, do you hear me?" With a playful titter, she elbowed him, and he came alert.

"You seem lost. Is something wrong?"

"Sorry, my dear Hen." He mustered a half-hearted chuckle. Then he actually looked at her, and his senses ignited.

Garbed in lavender wool, the customary ladies accouterment struck him as unremarkable, at first glance. Upon further inspection, the riding habit boasted vibrant blooms that appeared hand-painted on the bodice and the cuffs of the sleeves, and the cut fit her feminine physique like a glove and emphasized her narrow waist and tempting curves. The matching hat boasted a perky white plume and begged for attention, as if anyone could ignore Henrietta Graham.

"Shall we depart?" Unaware of his timorous state, she blinked and favored him with a glimpse of the endearing dimple on her left cheek.

"You are beautiful, Hen." If not for her father's presence, Ernest would have taken her in his arms and kissed her. Instead, he grabbed her by the wrist and tugged her in his wake, as he marched outside.

In the stable yard, he spared not a word, as he lifted her to the sidesaddle. Once she was settled, he gained his mount, turned toward the path that led to the limestone dales, and heeled the flanks of his stallion.

The cold breeze sliced through his hair, as he set a blazing pace, and his lady urged the mare faster. Side by side, they charged the dirt path, winding their way through the thick foliage, laughing as they rode. At last, he ducked to evade a low-lying branch and soared, as the landscape yielded to the resplendent valley, until they approached the lea, where he slowed his horse.

"Do you remember the time I fell, while attempting to secure a cluster of cowslips?" He pointed to the steep ravine. "You wanted them to adorn your coif."

"I was seven, but do not put the blame on my shoulders." She giggled, and how he had missed that sound. "If you recall, I warned you not to risk it, as did Barrington and Florence, but you insisted."

"Because I would do anything for you." Despite the carefree air, something functioned as a seemingly insurmountable hurdle between them, and he would have a full accounting, because he had so many questions, yet one occupied him to the exclusivity of all else. Drawing to a halt, he snagged her lead. "Why did you leave me?"

"But I did no such thing." All of a sudden, her shimmering visage broke, and tears welled in her brown eyes. "Why did you not bid me farewell, when my father sent me away? I searched and searched for you, but you never came to me. So when I arrived in Kent, I faithfully dispatched letters, every week, then every month, until I gave up, because I could not bear the absence of any return missive. Is that any way to treat a friend? Did I mean nothing to you?"

"I knew nothing of your departure, until you were gone, and I never received any letters. But I would have you know I wrote to you. Like you, I composed notes, which I gave to my father to frank, every week, until he sent me to Eton." As a soldier on post, he spent countless hours on guard for a messenger, always hoping that each new day might bring him word of his little bird, but his prayers went unanswered, and it amazed him how much it still hurt, after so many years had passed. "Had I known of your impending departure, I would have protested, as you were my Hen. You were my little bird."

"As you can see, I am no longer little." Oh, he could see plenty, as she sniffed, and he admired the swanlike curve of her neck. "And I was but a girl of eight. How could I refuse Papa's command, given it was so sudden, and I had no chance to delay? He sent me to Tunbridge Wells, to live with my aunt and uncle, because he said I needed a mother's influence. Did you expect me to defy him?"

"No." In truth, he wanted her to be happy, even if that happiness was predicated on his absence. Still, they were together, again, were they not? "Were you happy there? Were they good to you?"

"Uncle Jasper was very kind. He loved to read, and he took an active interest in my education. Sadly, he died of a fever, two years after I arrived." After pulling a lace-edged handkerchief from her pocket, she daubed her nose. "By far, the best part of my experience was working in Aunt Charlotte's dress shop."

"Oh?" As they did when they were children, they twined their fingers while they advanced at a slow gait, and the meager connection did much to warm him. "Is that where you procured your charming attire, as you are quite stunning?"

"Actually, I made what I am wearing." With unmasked pride, she lifted her chin, in an affectation he well remembered. "The design is my signature creation, featuring hand-painted flowers, and my skills were well known and rather in demand, in town."

"Do you mean to tell me that you sew?" In that instant, he studied the expertly made cuff and elegant style. "That you are in trade?"

"I am, indeed," she replied with gusto and more than a little pride, which he adored. "Does that shock you?"

"Given your well-known preference for all things frilly and flowery?" He snorted and tore his gaze from her ample bosom. "No. But I am surprised by your ingenuity, and you are obviously very talented."

"Thank you." If only he could stop obsessing over her mouth.

"I kissed you, yesterday." Why in the bloody hell did he have to remind her of his err in polite decorum?

"Did you?" Ah, she teased him.

"I will not apologize." Oh, no. Never would he express regret for that priceless treat.

"I expect not." Hen stiffened her spine. "And I do not require it."

"I will do it again." Ernest stole a side-glance and discovered her watching him.

Again, she favored him with her flirty dimple, as she canted her head. "Oh, I would hope so."

In that instant, he burst into laughter.

"It is so good to have you home." He nudged his stallion closer to her mare and brought Hen's gloved hand to his lips. "I missed you, more than you will ever know."

"And I missed you." To his relief, she met him halfway, as he leaned toward her, and they shared a tender kiss. "My sweet Ernest, was it so easy to forget me?"

"What do you mean?" He caressed her cheek and claimed another kiss. "I could never forget you."

"But you did not recognize me, when I landed in your lap." The anguish in her expression struck him as a punch to the gut. "Yet, I knew you from the moment you called to me."

"Dear Hen, you mistake devastating grief, which led me to bury my memories of you, for indifference." In frustration, he drew rein, jumped from the saddle, lifted her to the ground, and pulled her into his arms. As he cradled her head, he kissed her hair. "When I lost you, I was shattered, and nothing has gone right without you, but I long ago accepted the fact that I would never see you, again, so I concealed all traces of you in my personal history, else I might not have survived. Yet, you were with me. You have always been with me, my little bird."

"Do you think you are the only one who suffered?" She nuzzled his chest and gripped fistfuls of his lapels. "Despite my youth, I yearned for you, as you were my knight in shining armor, but I could not disobey my father. And I grieved, oh, how I mourned, as did you."

In some sort of wretched self-torment, he evoked an array of convoluted vignettes, Hen screaming, clawing, resisting, as her father dragged her to a traveling coach, while Ernest kicked her sire's shins, none of which he could reconcile with the kind stablemaster.

"How could he do that to us?" Relentless agony assailed Ernest, as he reflected on her absence, and he mulled what might have been, had she not been stolen from him. "For years, I was lost. With you gone, I ventured into these woods, desperate for any connection to you, however fleeting. And I counted the days, imagining that when I arrived at a certain date, you would return to me. But each successive disappointment chipped away at my resolve, until I surrendered to the misery and yielded any memory of you to the most wretched parts of my soul, that I might persist."

"I used to conjure visions of you, to keep me company, especially when I was afraid." Shifting in his arms, she positioned herself perfectly to receive another kiss, and he lingered, as he savored her intoxicating flesh, until she wrenched free. "Oh, Ernest, I was so alone without you."

Given her distress, he speared his fingers in the hair at her nape, pulled her impossibly close, and took her mouth in a bruising kiss. She could have resisted. Could have retreated. He would have honored her withdrawal, but instead she parted her lips and beckoned with a flick of her tongue, and Ernest unleashed the desire he had been holding in check for so long.

~

After a few blissful, heated, achingly desperate minutes, Ernest ended their kiss, but he kept Hen firmly anchored in his embrace, and that was just fine with her, as she clung to him and shivered with the unspent passion he provoked.

"What was that?" She swallowed hard and hugged him about the waist, because nothing they shared as children compared to what she experienced, in that moment. "What happened to us?"

"I was just wondering the same thing." He chuckled and tightened his grip. "But I know that I will never again let you part from me."

"All right." In light of her quick response, he chuckled and released her.

"Come." With a shrug, he doffed his heavy

coat, spread it on the ground, and led her to sit. After plopping beside her, he scooted closer and draped an arm about her shoulders, just as he did when they were young. "It is striking that, even after all this time, I still know you better than I know myself."

"Is it not?" She shook her head and marveled at the truth of his statement. Did he wonder, as did she, about their respective fates had they remained at Garring Manor? "Even now, I feel as though I can anticipate your every move, as if I could complete your sentences, because our thoughts remain in perfect alignment."

"Just like when we were children." Furrowing his brow, he compressed his lips. "Despite everything that has happened to me, despite what I endured in your absence, you remind me of the person I aspired to be, of the man I would be, for you."

"What troubles you?" How she ached for the bright, energetic boy she once knew, because the grown Ernest appeared a shadow of his former self. Indeed, he seemed broken and sad. "What did your father do to you, in my absence?"

"How did you—of course, you would know." Averting his gaze, he picked up a stick and stabbed at the ground. "You know how he treated me." When she nodded, he sighed. "It got much worse after your departure. Although I will never quite understand his motives, he drove me even harder than before, sometimes resorting to violence to achieve his means. Yet he always insisted he was doing it for my benefit. Needless to say, I did not shed a tear when he died."

"I am so sorry I was not here to support you." Cupping his cheek, she turned him to face her. "But I am here now, and I will always be your friend."

"Is that what we are? Friends?" He frowned. "There was a time when I would have been rather more than that."

"But we were playmates, and you did not expect Barrington to choose me as his partner for lady of the manor, when he was smitten with Lady Florence, even then." At one point, they made a pact to live in a neighboring estate and raise their offspring, together, as the fearless foursome. Of course, that was just a childish notion. "Do you claim an attachment, after these eleven years?"

"What if I do?" Suddenly, he pounced, and she found herself pinned by six feet of aroused male, yet she feared him not, because he was her Ernest. "What if I would realize our dream?"

"What are you saying?" Dare she hope? Did he cherish the same future she coveted? The one that included her, Ernest, and a house filled with children?

"Oh, I think you know." With that, he bent his head and claimed her mouth, and then Henrietta could not form a single coherent response.

Unprepared for the sheer, undeniable force of his ardor, and too inexperienced to resist, she gave herself without restraint and uttered no protest, when he set his palm to her breast. Strange and altogether foreign sensations sparked and lanced through her, as he pressed on her caresses she could not quite interpret. Heat poured through her veins, and her ears rang a carillon of excitement, when he loosened the bodice of her riding habit and slipped his hand inside, to cup her bare flesh.

Pushing hard, she came up for air. "Ernest, do not play with my affection. What are your intentions?"

"We need to form a plan, and I must talk with my brother." Sitting upright, he counted a list on his fingers. "First, I want you to move to the main house, as the stable yard is not an appropriate place for you to live, given what I have in mind. Second, I want to give

you a London season and a come-out ball."
Then he grew quiet. "After a month, we will
post the banns, which will give us ample
opportunity to reacquaint ourselves, though I
submit that is unnecessary, and we can marry
at St. George's in Hanover Square, with the
best of society in attendance."

"Are you mad?" For a few minutes,
Henrietta feared she might swoon, and she
slumped to the side, as his words echoed in
her brain. "We have not seen each other in
eleven years, and we are just reunited. How
can you offer for me, with any sincerity?"

"Because I am the same person who
adored you, so long ago, my little bird." He
tipped her chin, bringing her gaze to his, and
she could lose herself in his blue eyes. It was
the determination in his stare that convinced
her of the truth in his candor. "And I wager
you feel the same about me."

"I do," she answered, without hesitation.
"As sure as I know my name, I do not doubt
you."

"Then let us return to Garring, as there is
much to be arranged, and I would not waste
another second." Ernest scrambled to his
feet, taking her with him. Then he dropped
to a knee, as he held her hands in his.
"Dearest Henrietta, my childhood love, my

little bird, will you consent to be my wife and make me the happiest man in the world? Will you bear my children and be my partner in all enterprises, for as long as we both shall live?"

"Yes." Of course, she should have known he would make a formal proposal, because he was anything if not proper. When he stretched upright, to seal their pact with another searing kiss, she uttered a silent prayer that she was not dreaming, because it appeared her fondest wish had, at long last, come true. "But I thought we were to tour the ancient yews."

"Not so, anymore, my lady." With palms at her hips, he lifted her to the saddle. "As I said, there is much to be done, and I would have you settled in a guest room, by this evening."

"What is the urgency?" Never had she seen him so focused and deliberate, and it did much to reassure her. Yet, his actions also flung her into a sea of uncertainty, because she remained a stablemaster's daughter, and he was a gentleman's son. "And have you spoken to my father?"

"Darling Hen, I have waited eleven years for this moment, so you cannot accuse me of rushing you to the altar." He leaped atop his stallion. "As for your father, I will talk to him after I discuss the matter with Barrington, as he is the head of the family." Then he flicked the reins. "*Yaa.*"

At full gallop, they retraced the path, and she studied Ernest's profile, as they drove their mounts harder and faster. Hints of the blithe boy invested his countenance, as he glanced at her, grinned, and winked, yet she struggled to draw breath, as everything seemed to spin out of control. By the time they trotted into the stable yard, countless questions plagued her.

"Ernest, there is no need for me to move my belongings, as I am quite content in my little room in the cabin." With infinite care, he pulled her from the mare. "Please, I would savor the events preceding our nuptials, because I never presumed it would happen, when I returned to Derbyshire."

"My dear, I will brook no refusal, as I want you near me, now and forever." In a scandalous display of familiarity, he kissed her in the yard, in full view of the hands—and her father. "I shall send two footmen to collect your things, so you should gather the items and be ready."

With that, he set her at arm's length, dipped his chin, and marched toward the main house, leaving her to confront her none-too-happy sire, as evidenced by the red flush in his cheeks and foreboding frown.

"Hello, Papa." She ignored his disapproving manner. "I have wonderful news to share."

"Henrietta Katherine, just what are you about, engaging in such shameless behavior in front of the servants?" Grabbing her by the elbow, he led her into a stall. "I will not have you cavorting with Lord Ernest, as some sort of low woman, because you are no rich man's courtesan, and hell will freeze before I allow it."

"But I am not cavorting with him." She rubbed her abused appendage and rued his harsh words, which belied a cruel assumption based on the difference of her birth—one she did not wish to confront. "Papa, the most amazing thing happened. Ernest asked me to marry him, and I accepted his proposal."

"*What?*" He pressed a clenched fist to his chest and then spat. "No. It is out of the question. I forbid it."

"Why?" Confused and alarmed by the vehemence of his response, she retreated a step. "What have you against Ernest?"

"He is of the noble class, and you are but a stablemaster's daughter. Believe me, it is not a good idea." Never had she seen her father so angry, as he wagged a finger in reproach. "You will not marry Lord Ernest. In fact, I think it best that you leave Derbyshire, as soon as I can arrange it. I have been saving a bit of money, and I could send you to Paris, to open a new boutique. You would like that, would you not?"

"Paris?" Stunned, she could scarcely organize her thoughts. "Papa, I am only just returned. Why would you send me away? And I mean to be Ernest's wife. Indeed, I am to move into the main house, today."

"No." Baring his teeth, he shook his head violently. "I will not allow it. You are my daughter, and I say where you do and do not live. Under no circumstances will I permit you to act as Lord Ernest's whore."

"How dare you speak to me thus." Hurt, she fought tears, because she expected her father to greet the joyous news in the same spirit with which she welcomed Ernest's proposal. "I care for Ernest, and he wants me. How could you deny me the chance to improve myself with a man who wants naught more than to grant my every desire?"

"Because so-called society will never accept you, regardless of Lord Ernest's good intentions." Papa averted his gaze and scowled. "They will treat you with disdain.

They will mock and shame you. They will cast you out and delight in your misery, because to them you will always be a stablemaster's daughter and nothing more."

"What need have I of their good opinion, when I have Ernest?" Despite her pretty words, her father seized upon the one concern that provoked a mountain of doubts, and as much as she hated to admit it, he was right. Still, Henrietta had to fight for what she wanted, and she wanted Ernest. "Dearest father, I love you, and I would never purposely disobey you. Rather, I would honor your wishes, but in this instance, I cannot. I must follow my heart, which knows no silly rules, and it lies with Ernest."

CHAPTER THREE

The study at Garring Manor had changed little since Ernest was a young boy, and it held no happy memories for him, because his father often chose that location to dispense discipline. As he crossed the threshold, his ears echoed with the telltale cries for mercy, which mingled with the sharp report of the leather belt, as it struck the bare flesh of his backside, and he shuddered and drained the glass of brandy his brother thrust into his hand.

"Ernest, are you all right?" Barrington carried a crystal decanter to the small table that perched between the two high-back chairs before the hearth. As he poured another healthy portion of the amber liquid into Ernest's brandy balloon, Barrington frowned. "You are quite pale."

"I was reflecting on our childhood and how much I detested being summoned to this room." And Ernest resented his brother's similar command, because it brought to mind the horrors he endured at their sire's hand. To his disgust, as he descended the stairs, his knees buckled more than once, and his palms dampened. In so many ways, he remained the frightened little boy, lost and alone, but not so anymore, because now he had Henrietta to comfort him, as she once did. "Why do you think our father hated me so much?"

"For what it is worth, I do not believe it was a matter of hate. While I know there is no excuse for his barbaric treatment of you, I suspect he did not know how to love you. Indeed, he did not know what to do with you." Gazing into the flames, Barrington shook his head. "Whereas I was his heir, thus he understood what was required of him, in respect to me, and he met the demands of rank but nothing more. We were never friends or drinking companions. He never invited me to White's. While I submit he was too easy on me, he knew not how to handle you, so he hurt you to make you a man, in his way."

"Thus he beat me for my own good, and I am supposed to believe that was love?" Pain nestled in Ernest's chest, and he cursed himself as tears formed in his eyes. Would he never escape the horrors of the past, or was he doomed to forever revisit the savagery that haunted his slumber, even as an adult? "No matter what you say, I will curse him until my death. Indeed, I would not spit on his grave were it on fire."

"I do not blame you, and you know. I tried to protect you." Barrington glanced at Ernest and frowned. "I tried to intervene on your behalf, and I begged him to stop."

"I remember well." He almost choked on the recollection, which only intensified his anguish. "Father called me a coward, accused me of soliciting your sympathy, and he whipped me that much longer and harder."

"After that, I was afraid to interfere, because I did not wish to cause you further suffering, but I have been on your side, since we wore short coats, little brother." Barrington shifted. "Which is why I did not protest, when Crawford informed me that you moved Henrietta into a guestroom."

"I was going to tell you, but the situation developed far faster than anticipated." Indeed, even Ernest did not quite know where to go, as he had not planned to offer for Hen, or any woman, when he returned to

Derbyshire, yet he did not hesitate when it came to his little bird. They had already lost eleven years, and he would not waste another minute. "But you cannot claim to be surprised, as you know I have always wanted Henrietta Graham, just as you pursued Florence. Is that why you did not tell me of her return?"

"To be honest, I was rather shocked by the revelations, but I recovered. As for her return, I wanted her to surprise you, because I know of your longstanding affinity, where she is concerned." Leaning against the armrest, Barrington propped an elbow and cradled his chin in his palm. "Still, have you any idea of the magnitude of issues you court?"

"Do you object?" Ernest gnashed his teeth. "Does Florence?"

"To Hen?" Barrington snorted. "No. And Florence was beside herself with joy, as you know she counts Hen a dear friend, as do I. We have known the stablemaster's daughter as long as you, and we were all playmates, so there is no objection here."

"Then what is the problem?" In truth, Ernest was not prepared to defend his position, because he only knew the ultimate goal. He would make Henrietta his wife. "Why do you take exception?"

"Come now." Barrington arched a brow. "You cannot be that naïve. What of the Season, when you journey to London?"

"You refer to the difference in our social status, of course." Ernest set aside the brandy, as he needed no liquid courage to confront that particular query. "But the circumstances of her birth do not signify, to me, because our devotion transcends such boundaries."

Indeed, his was a masterful bit of trickery, to amass his fears, his anxieties, his insecurities, his doubts—his need to evade and deny them, and out of those shattered remnants of misery and pain to construct an invincible suit of armor with which to face the world, with Henrietta firmly planted at his side. And within that world, he would carve out a secret place for the two of them, where they could create their own future, without fear of recrimination.

"It will matter to society, and therein lies the problem." As usual, Barrington highlighted the singular snare in Ernest's plans, with unerring accuracy. "I know you. Although I can afford to thumb my nose at the *ton*, as I am a marquess, you enjoy no such luxury, and you have always valued their good opinion. To them, what you propose is forbidden, and what are you without their respect?"

"You think I have not considered that? You think me ignorant of the piety and self-righteous rationalizations construed by society to forbid something that is not wrong, in the first place? I submit Henrietta is not of low birth. Rather, she is a victim of those who would control her." The mere thought of surrendering Hen and wedding someone else evoked a violent response, and he would not even contemplate the prospect, now that they were reunited. "But I cannot be deterred, brother. I want Hen. I have never wanted anything as much as I want her, and I will have her, with or without your blessing."

"Wait a minute." Barrington stiffened his spine. "Do not include me in that perfumed pack of wolves, because I am the last person to cast stones, given I took up piracy while on the run." Then he stood, walked to his desk, opened a drawer, sifted through various items, and returned with an official looking document. "If you intend to see this through, then you should know all the facts."

Curious, Ernest snatched the paper from his brother's grasp and perused what turned out to be a contract between their sire and the stablemaster. As he digested the contents of the agreement, his fingers shook, and he made no attempt to hide the tears that flowed freely down his cheeks, given the gravity of the terms.

"I will *never* forgive him for this." It was the final insult, and he slumped his shoulders, as the depth of the betrayal weighed heavy. In a sense, it was as though he lost Henrietta all over again.

Since that horrible day when he first learned of her departure, he suffered her absence repeatedly, as manifested by even the smallest most innocent detail. He experienced her loss in the breeze that blew through the meadow where they often played, in the cowslips that returned every spring, in the empty space where she often sat on the front porch of the stablemaster's cottage, waiting for him, and the old yew she loved to climb.

He did not lose her just once.

He lost her countless times, in incalculable ways, over and over again, such that the torment often seemed never-ending.

"He knew what she meant to me, even then. Yet he conspired to take away the one person who gave me hope, and he paid her father a vast deal more than generous annuity to achieve his aims." He gave vent to an unholy roar of disgust. "And I am to be disinherited and removed from the line of succession, should something happen to you and your heir, if I marry Hen."

"No." With feet firmly planted, Barrington folded his arms. "When our father died, and the title and estate came into my possession, our solicitor notified me of the stipulations of the entailment, and I altered them, as was my right, but the annuity remains in effect, as I would not jeopardize Hen's financial security."

"Why would you do that?" Ernest drew a handkerchief from his coat pocket and wiped his face. "Why do you care?"

"Because it was wrong, and if our father was here, at this very moment, I would tell him so." Barrington rested a hand to Ernest's shoulder. "Whatever you decide to do with your life is your affair, and I will support you in your cause, come what may. However, if you insist on taking Hen as your bride, you had better commit, wholeheartedly, because the task will not be easy for either of you, and it will be doubly hard on her."

"What do you mean?" Reeling from the treachery, Ernest again emptied his glass.

"If you will ponder the situation with your customary attention to detail, you will comprehend my warning, provided you start thinking with your brain and not with your breeches." Barrington chucked Earnest's chin. "Men may be the stronger sex, but women rule London's ballrooms, and the *grand dames* can be vicious, especially when it becomes clear that another eligible bachelor is checked off their list of potential targets. When they discover your bride-to-be is the daughter of our stablemaster, things are liable get ugly."

"Then I must take care that they never find out her true history, else I may be moved to violence in her defense. I must compose a new account to satisfy the gossips and protect my lady." All manner of narratives came to life, as Ernest reflected on the possibilities, and he plotted a course with unbending detail. He would persist, he would fight, he would claw his way back to that part of his life stolen from him by his unscrupulous father and find a measure of happiness. That he would triumph with Henrietta despite his father's meddling would be the sweetest victory of all. "First, I must pay a visit to our stablemaster, assure him that my intentions are honorable, and secure his approval, else I am doomed to failure."

~

Sunlight filtered through the drapes, as

Henrietta languished in the plush four-poster of a guestroom at Garring Manor. Decorated in rich blue damask, trimmed in old gold, with refined mahogany furnishings in the Sheraton tradition, the chamber suited her tastes. Stretching, she hummed her appreciation of the soft sheets and then scooted to the edge of the mattress, just as a maid entered the room.

"Good morning, Miss Graham." Maisy, a particularly young servant, curtseyed. "Crawford assigned me to attend your needs. Shall I air a dress and style your hair?"

"But that is too ridiculous, and since when do you address me so formally?" Was it Henrietta's imagination, or did she detect a note of sarcasm in Maisy's tone? "I am perfectly capable of managing myself."

"Sorry, Miss Graham." Maisy yanked the counterpane none too gently, as she made the bed. "I have my orders, and I will do my duty, even for a stablemaster's daughter who would pass herself off as a lady."

"I beg your pardon?" It was the first signal that not everyone would cheer Hen's new position in the household, and she marked her father's prophetic words. While she anticipated some resistance from the debutantes, never had she expected discord from her own rank. What awaited her in London, amid polite society unaccustomed to marriage between the classes? "If you are assigned to perform my bidding, then you are dismissed."

"Fine." Maisy dropped a pillow and curtseyed. "Have a pleasant day, Miss Graham."

Angry and more than a little hurt by the exchange, Henrietta donned a morning dress of her own design, in a pale pink muslin, with hand-painted flowers at the hem, the cuffs of the sleeves, and the neckline. After arranging her hair in a severe chignon, to match her mood, she pulled her wool pelisse from the armoire and stomped into the hall. At the landing, she spied a familiar and welcomed face.

"Florence—I mean, Marchioness Ravenwood." Hen sketched a quick curtsey, and with outstretched arms they met and shared a warm hug. "It is wonderful to see you, and I congratulate you on your wedding, the birth of your son, and the joyous news of the impending addition to your family."

"Stuff and nonsense, as I have always been Florence to you, dear Hen, my friend, although I would argue you are a sister to me, and I am so happy you are home." The noblewoman laughed and kissed Henrietta's cheek. "And thank you, so much. I was thrilled when Barrington told me of your engagement to Ernest, and you must let me throw you the most extravagant wedding London has ever seen. We will post the banns, I shall take out an announcement in *The Times*, and you will walk the aisle at St. George's. Can you just imagine it? It will be as we fantasized, when we were young."

"That would be lovely." Suddenly, the full weight of Henrietta's decision struck her as a blow to the face, and she stumbled to the side, as she pondered what Ernest's plan demanded of her. "*Oh.*"

"Hen, are you all right?" As usual, Florence provided unshakeable support. "You are white as a sheet." She led Henrietta to a bench in the gallery. "Come and sit."

"I do not know what is wrong with me." Surrounded by the disapproving gazes of Ernest's ancestors, depicted in paint and plaster, which seemed to cry out in protest, for all eternity, Hen fanned herself and then pressed a clenched fist to her mouth. In so short a span of time, she measured her existence in terms of absence, by the empty spaces she once inhabited, instinctively reaching for them as a hungry babe sought its mother's breast. In a sense, she felt trapped between two worlds, such that neither place offered sanctuary, and it had only been one night, yet, she belonged nowhere. "I apologize, as I am not myself."

"It could not be that you attempt to do too much, at once." Florence made a show of studying the ceiling and then met Hen's stare. "Because you would never do that."

Together, they burst into laughter.

"How I missed you, Flo." At last, Henrietta found an ally, and she needed one just then. "Two days ago, when Ernest and I reunited, everything seemed so clear. Although I had not seen or spoken to him in eleven years, it was as if we never parted. When he proposed, I accepted him with no reservations."

"And now that you have slept on it, you realize things are a bit more complicated?" Florence had a way with reducing the complexities of life to their simplest form, something Henrietta appreciated. "Talk to me."

"I know not what came over me." When Florence arched a brow, Hen sighed. "Oh, all right. Ernest kissed me, everything went hazy, and I suspect I would have surrendered to Boney, at that point."

"Your first love." Florence closed her eyes and exhaled. "How enticing and delicious." Then she came alert. "So, how was it?"

"It was magical." Henrietta clutched her throat and revisited the cherished memory. "As many times as I engaged in such behavior with him, in my dreams, it was nothing compared to the real thing."

"Is that when he proposed?" Florence inquired. "Barrington told me of Ernest's plans."

"Am I a fool for accepting him?" Henrietta reflected on Maisy's reaction to Hen's new status. "I do not believe everyone wishes me well."

"What did you expect?" Florence's statement cut Hen to her marrow. "While this may be eighteen-nineteen, there are some institutions that remain firmly entrenched in English society, and you must either overcome or ignore the naysayers, and I suspect there will be many, so you must prepare yourself for the fight, and it will be a fight."

"Am I wrong for wanting Ernest?" Hen gulped. "Do I aim too high?"

"Do you truly want him?" Flo twined her fingers in Hen's.

"He is the only man I have ever wanted."

Yet, from where Henrietta stood, she could not seize upon a solution that would enable her to marry Ernest and maintain her dignity. Something had to give, but what was she willing to surrender to claim the man she always wanted? "But at what cost will I break the dictates of society, and what will it do to Ernest?"

"Did Ernest share the details of Barrington's exile?" When Hen nodded the affirmative, Florence bowed her head. "There are those who shunned me during my husband's absence, after the authorities accused him of a murder he did not commit. While he was on the run, he resorted to piracy, to survive, and he required a pardon from the Crown to return to England." She squeezed Hen's hand. "During those lonely, miserable days, I prayed for Barrington's safety and confined myself to my residence. I relied on my family for comfort, but even my father abandoned me, in some respects, and society, aided and abetted by my so-called friends, ran my name through the muck, if only to satisfy their insatiable lust for scandal and blood."

"Ernest said he offered for you, but you feigned illness to forestall the nuptials." Hen could not begin to comprehend what her childhood companion endured at the hands of those who should have championed her. "Of course, he explained he did so out of desperation, in order to defend you, because he knew not if Barrington would ever come home. I wish I had been there for you."

"In some respects, you were, because I relied on fond memories of our friendship to sustain me in the darkest hours, and of that there were many." Florence hugged her belly and smiled. "I am sure you know I have nothing against Ernest, but I could not wed him, when my heart has always belonged to Barrington, and that is why you must not yield the field. No matter what anyone says, you must be strong and win your man, because love knows no social boundaries." She clucked her tongue. "Given how the *ton* treated me, they may go to the devil."

"*Florence*." Henrietta giggled and then started at the sound of approaching male voices, as she was unprepared to confront the Howe brothers. "I should go."

"Will you not break your fast with the family?" Florence brushed the backs of her knuckles to Hen's cheek. "We are stronger, together. And we would help you make the transition into society."

"I need to speak with my father, and I

should take care of his morning meal, despite my new status." Hen pondered his objection to her wedding and frowned. As she recalled their quarrel, her spirits sank. "He does not support me."

"That is because he belongs to an older generation, much like my father, and they are set in their ways." Florence averted her gaze. "And there are those who will oppose you, if for no other reason than to take fiendish satisfaction in your pain, while still others will protest because they envy you. And some simply prefer to keep you low, that they might elevate themselves." She shrugged. "Ultimately, who knows why people do what they do, but you cannot be discouraged."

"You are right." With renewed resolve, Hen stood and smoothed her skirts. "And although I appreciate the invitation to breakfast, I shall instead join my father and try to mend our differences, because, whether or not he likes it, I need him on my side."

"A wise decision, but I expected nothing less." Flo rose from the bench. "But I would correct you in one respect." She wagged a finger. "This is now your home, we are your family, and you require no invitation to dine with us. When you are ready, we must go shopping, to arm you for the *ton's* ballrooms, and you must be perfect."

"All right." Henrietta inhaled a deep, calming breath, strolled to the landing, checked for any sign of Ernest, and ran down the stairs. In the foyer, she veered right and sprinted along the hall. In the back parlor, she slipped beyond the terrace doors.

After crossing the garden, she skipped into the yard. Since it was early, only a few hands went about their duties, cleaning stalls, feeding horses, and polishing saddles. A single light shone through the front window of the little cottage she shared with her father, and she climbed the steps. Unsure of her welcome, as she reached for the knob, she paused. Instead, she knocked.

With an expression of surprise, her father set wide the heavy panel. "Henrietta, what are you doing here?"

"I wish to talk, Papa." When she noted the dark circles and lines of strain etched about his eyes, she regretted their disagreement. "I would make peace, if you permit it, as I hate being at odds with you."

"My dear child, I only want what is best for you." In an instant, he pulled her into his reassuring embrace, and she savored the comforting and familiar scent of his shaving soap. "You are all I have left in the world, and I would protect you from harm."

"I am so sorry we argued." As the tension abated, she shed a few tears and sniffed. "May I cook your breakfast, and you could help me plan my future?"

"I would love that." Papa kissed her hair. "Come inside, and warm yourself, as it is a cold morning."

In quiet, Hen retrieved a cast-iron pan and placed it atop a burner on the wood burning range, while her father collected the dishes. After tending the firebox, she stoked a roaring blaze. Fried kippers filled the small abode with a tempting aroma, and she scrambled eggs and toasted a few slices of bread, as tea steeped in a chipped porcelain pot.

As she assumed her place at the table that marked so many happy childhood memories, even her father appeared to have relaxed. In silence, they shared the meal. Then he cleared his throat, and she braced.

"Although you have accepted Lord Ernest's proposal of marriage, it does not follow that you must wed him." Papa rested his elbows atop the table and steepled his hands. "Please, hear me out, and then you may have your say. You do not know this, but I have saved a substantial sum of money, enough to afford you a brand-new start, in a place of your choosing, should you have need of it. You can go anywhere you desire. You need not stay here and grovel for scraps of approval from upper ranks."

"Papa, I mean to be Ernest's wife." She quieted when he raised a finger.

"I understand that, but it may not come to pass, and I would not have you believe you have no other options." As he gazed at his empty plate, he seemed to age ten years, and she rued the distress she caused him. "In some respects, I have always known you did not belong in the stables. Yet, I am not sure you belong in the manor house, either. But you were happy, in trade, and you are a master with a needle and thread, as your aunt boasted of your talents, so why would you waste your potential?" He leaned in her direction. "You could make your own way, on your terms, Henrietta. Beholden to none, you can be whatever you choose to be, rather than some ornament for a wealthy man. Perhaps, you could find someone from your class to take as a husband, because I would never have you bow to those who consider you beneath them, when they are not fit to wipe the mud from your boots."

"Am I to understand you no longer object to my engagement?" Indeed, it seemed he acquiesced, thus her troubles were no more, and she could have shouted for joy. "You will give us your blessing, if I ask it of you?"

Before he could answer, Ernest barged into the cottage.

"Graham, I have come to formally offer for your daughter." Ernest tossed a piece of parchment at her father. "I know of the contract you settled with the previous Lord Ravenwood, and I would be willing to transfer the annuity into your name, in exchange for your permission to wed Henrietta."

"What contract?" Befuddled, she blinked and then snatched the paper from her father's grasp, as he stammered. A quick scan of the contents left her reeling, as it detailed an unforgiveable conspiracy to keep her from Ernest. But it was her father's involvement that struck the most vicious blow, and she flew into the kitchen, where she bent and vomited into a bucket.

"Are you all right?" When she nodded, Ernest knelt at her side and offered his handkerchief. "You did not know of the arrangement our parents orchestrated, to keep us apart."

It was a statement, not a question.

She needed to cry, but she would go to her grave before indulging in such humiliating behavior in front of Ernest. Hiking her skirts, she rushed along the short corridor, where her father loomed, and she drew up short. "Do not touch me."

With a sorrowful expression, he splayed his arms. "Henrietta, please, I can explain."

"What, Father? Exactly what can you explain?" In that very instant, something inside her shattered, as a much-cherished illusion died. Her father had always been her champion. Her protector. And it was a lie. The tears rolled down her cheeks, but she cared not, as she wanted him to witness the anguish he inflicted upon her. "How you abandoned me in favor of Lord Ravenwood? How you packed me up and sent me to Kent? How you sold me into trade for three hundred pounds a year? You accuse Ernest of trying to alter my nature, but you are the one who betrayed me. You disgust me, because you have become that which you protest."

With that, she darted around the table, wrenched open the door, and fled toward the north fields.

CHAPTER FOUR

There were moments in Ernest's life when he faced seemingly insurmountable obstacles, insuperable barriers that brought lesser men to their knees, only to recover and retrench after a few quiet minutes of reflection, because he was particularly adept at managing crises. That was his talent. As he stood in the tense aftermath of Henrietta's fiery rebuke, that was not one of those moments, and he was at a loss as to how he could recover.

"Why could you not leave her be?" The grave tone of Graham's query hit Ernest squarely between the eyes. "She was happy in Kent, without you."

Trying but failing to ignore the unmistakable ire in the stablemaster's voice, Ernest shuddered. "I should go after her."

"Can you not leave well enough alone?" Graham rested his head in his hands. "My daughter is not for you."

"Why did you conspire with my father to keep Hen and I apart? Were we so wrong for each other? What have you against me?" Ernest bristled beneath the old man's stare, which did not waver beneath his caustic queries. "Is it my rank or my wealth that bothers you?"

"Both." The stablemaster's look sent a chill down Ernest's spine. "My daughter is no lady, by society's standards, and she brings naught but the clothes on her back to any union, but still you could never deserve her, given you have been pampered and spoiled from the cradle."

"Have care how you speak, because you know nothing of my upbringing." He could have laughed at the irony, given the brutal reality. But that was the cruelest part of the abuse he suffered at his father's hands. In a sense, Ernest manifested the worst, most shameful aspect of his sire, and yet he protected his father, by maintaining the secrecy surrounding the beatings. At once, he represented the scene of the horrible savagery and its concealment, which only compounded the torture. Why did he do it? Why maintain the secrecy? Because his father warned of the damage the truth would cause the family, and everyone would blame Ernest. Although his father had been gone more than seven years, the man still tormented Ernest. "And do you think I do not know that I could spend my life endeavoring to perform noble deeds, end universal suffering, and bring about world peace, and I could not equal her worth? But I care for her. As I come from less than humble beginnings, there are not many things I need, but I need her. I can give her everything her heart desires, and I pledge to do so, if you will but give us a chance."

"Sit down, Lord Ernest." The stablemaster kicked out a chair. "Let Henrietta have her cry, as I suspect we have disappointed her, and then you may pursue her." He wiped his face with his hand and compressed his lips. "Tell me why you are so set on marrying my girl, when you could have any woman of your choosing."

"Because she wants me." It was too late when Ernest comprehended how that sounded, and he huffed in frustration. "What I mean is she wanted me before she knew anything of titles, social standing, and personal riches. Have you any idea what that means to a person in my position?"

"But you were children, too young to possess any real understanding of emotional attachment and commitment." Wide-eyed, Graham's incredulity was not lost on Ernest. "How can you honestly claim, with any certainty, that she is destined to be your mate, for eternity, given you just returned to Derbyshire and have not seen her in eleven years? Because I will accept nothing less than what she deserves, when it comes to Henrietta."

"Age does not signify, when it comes to affairs of the heart." In that instant, Ernest evoked sweet reflections of the heated tryst he shared with Hen, in the back parlor. Yes, he took liberties that were not his to own, but she resisted not, and he could not restrain himself, when she was so accommodating. Despite their extended separation, the long, tender kisses, the intimate caresses, and the hour passed in her arms indicated a prevailing allegiance he could not—would not disregard. "Believe me, the attraction remains, and it is stronger than ever."

"And you would wed her, in full view of society, proclaiming for all to see that you have taken a lowborn bride?" Graham pounded a fist to the table. "That is what they will deuced call her, and I cannot abide it."

"Not if I invent an alternate narrative." An idea occurred to Ernest, and he snapped his fingers. "What if we tell everyone she is a distant cousin? Not to hide the truth, because I do not give a damn about her origins, but to protect her?" In desperation, he reached across the table and grasped the stablemaster's wrist. "I am begging you. Name your terms, ask any price, because I must have Henrietta as my wife."

"What if she decides otherwise?" The pedestrian query, innocently posed, was enough to strike fear in Ernest's heart, because he had not let himself consider the possibility. "What if my daughter refuses to live a lie, as that is what you require of her? I have saved a sum of money that will offer her a fresh start, far away from you. In another place, she could be whatever she wants. How do you know she will obey your request, in the face of such an opportunity?"

"Because I know her better than I know myself, and she will do it, if I ask it of her. If I explain it is for her own good, with so much hanging in the balance, she will cooperate." Myriad ideas flittered through his brain, and he seized upon anything that supported his position. In seconds, a scheme took shape, and he nurtured and tended it. "We can create a persona, complete with a backstory to satisfy even the nosiest gossipmonger. And I will give her a season unlike any other, dress her in the finest gowns, and secure invitations to the most exclusive parties. By the time I am finished, Henrietta will be the envy of every debutante in London, and then she will walk the aisle at St. George's."

"But she will not be herself. She will be something else." Her father retreated and toyed with a dirty napkin. "Do you not see? Are you that blind?" Graham scowled. "You would force her to become what she is not, and what would you do with her, then? Would you not grow tired of her?"

"No, that is not true, because I care for her." Ernest waved dismissively, as everything inside him rebelled at the mere suggestion. "That will never happen, because Hen is too strong, and you underestimate her."

"Perhaps you idealize the situation, to my daughter's disservice. You draw conclusions to suit your needs, with my daughter's happiness in the balance." The stablemaster bared his teeth, and Ernest sat back in his chair. "Regardless of your assumptions, the classes should not mix. In that, your father and I were in complete agreement."

"Is that why you signed my father's contract, which took Henrietta from me?" Not for a minute would Ernest relent, when he was so close to winning his prize. "Still, she will not be deterred. She literally fell into my lap. Are you so invested in societal dictates that you refuse to recognize the fact that your daughter wants to be with me? Will you not consider what she desires?"

Silence weighed heavy in the modest cottage.

At last, Graham heaved a mournful sighed. "Lord Ernest, I remain in the employ of your family, and I have never brought dishonor upon my position. What I have done, I did for my daughter's sake, and nothing more. That aside, what would you have of me?"

"Sir, I mean no disrespect, but I am no young lad, and I will not let her go without a fight. You may discount our devotion, but Henrietta and I are bound by a power I cannot begin to describe. I only know it exists." Clenching his fists at his sides, Ernest prayed for calm. "Your arrangement with my father is ended, and he is no more. Now let us discuss the matter like gentlemen, but heed my warning, and make no mistake, because I will not leave here without your permission to wed Henrietta. One way or another, she will be my wife."

~

After drying the last of her tears, Henrietta strolled to the small, fenced graveyard tucked behind the little estate chapel, which nestled beneath the thick canopy of a cluster of massive yews. Kneeling, she pulled a few brown weeds and cleared some rocks from her mother's final resting place. So often, she wondered how her life would have been different, had her mother survived Hen's birth.

In that moment, given all the tumult, she desperately needed her mother.

"How I wish I had known you." Were it spring, she would have collected a bouquet of wildflowers to give to the woman who brought Henrietta into the world. "I have so many questions, and I have no one to ask. Papa broke faith with me, and Ernest wishes to marry me. How I need your sage advice, Mama."

Telltale hoofbeats signaled the arrival Hen anticipated, and she glanced in the general direction of the path, as Ernest drew rein and jumped from the saddle. He was right. He knew her better than she knew herself, and in some respects that terrified her. Thus, her first instinct was to run, but she stood and held her ground.

"Forgive me, sweetheart." With a wild yet contrite expression, he charged her. As he pulled her into his arms, he bent his head and kissed her forehead. "I did not know you were unaware of the pact between our two fathers. Indeed, when I learned of it, I thought you complicit."

"And why would I know of it, given I was but eight years old and lacked the maturity to understand such things?" To her dismay, the tears returned with a vengeance, and she sobbed. "Oh, Ernest, how could they do that to us? Was I so wrong for you? Did they think me a threat?"

"According to your father, they sought to spare us the pain of eventual separation and heartbreak, owing to society's predictable refusal to accept us." After shifting her in his grasp, he cupped her cheek and pressed his lips to hers. "But I care not for the *ton's* good opinion, as you are far more important to me."

"Then what do we do, because it seems as if the whole world is against us, and we have yet to begin the fight." In desperation, she gripped the lapels of his coat and sniffed. "Even the servants treat me with disdain."

"What?" With a violent flinch, he set her at arm's length. "Who abused you?"

"It is nothing." Unwilling to cause trouble, more than she had already, she clamped shut her mouth, as she should have said nothing.

"Henrietta, tell me who hurt you, and I shall dismiss them, this instant." When she shook her head and remained mute, he lowered his chin. "Give me the name, or I will fire the entire household of domestics, with my brother's full support, because it is not their place to judge me, the company I keep, or my chosen bride."

In light of his dire warning, which she doubted not, she sighed.

"It was Maisy." In that moment, Hen cursed herself for mentioning the problem. "But what do you intend? Will you discharge everyone who offends me?"

"If necessary, yes." Given his rigid stance, she did not doubt him, and she adored his determination. "And you must defend your new station, else you will never succeed."

"Do you not see that would only foster more discontent among the servants? And what of those you do not employ?" Splaying her fingers across his chest, she tried but could not muster outrage at the audacity of his position, because she loved his protective nature. "Will you call them out, in some sort of misplaced sense of chivalry? You and I both know we cannot force people to receive me in my new capacity."

"Actually, we may be able to achieve just that, if you will but hear my plan." His sly smile beckoned, as he swept her off her feet, carried her to his stallion, lifted her to the saddle, and then joined her. "I made a fair and equitable gentleman's agreement, with your father's blessing, so let us tour the north fields and plot our next move."

"What if we embark on a fool's errand that will end in naught but ruin and despair?" As he pulled her sideways, into his lap, she folded her arms and shivered, when he pressed flirty little kisses along the crest of her ear. "You cannot seduce your way out of this, Ernest. I would have your answer. Are you prepared to lose?"

"Yes." The single word, uttered in a low, gravelly voice rocked her, as he seemed so casual about their future. "But it will not come to that. At least, I hope it will not come to that."

"Then what have you in mind?" Resting against his stalwart frame, she braced for the news. "And does my father truly support us, or did you use your influence to pressure him?"

"My dear, you do not give me much credit, as I would never resort to coercion to achieve my aim, especially when it comes to you." As the cool breeze rustled her hair, he steered the horse down the narrow path. "Rather, your father and I agree that your happiness is of paramount importance. Indeed, you are all that matters, so he will accept your decision, as will I. In fact, I promised him I would not challenge you, should you opt for something, or someone, else."

"What does that mean?" How could he think, for even a minute, that she would want someone else, when she dreamed of a life with Ernest, for as long as she could remember? Was he prepared to surrender before the challenge began? "Do you not want me?"

"Darling Hen, for me, you are everything." Cupping her chin, he extended comfort in a kiss. "But what we are about to embark upon is not for the faint of heart, as it will not be easy. Society defines our relationship as forbidden, so we must be strong, if we are to succeed. However, with a minor alteration, harmless in the grand scheme, we might outwit the scandalmongers and win the future we desire."

"What minor alteration?" Puzzled by his curious comment, she pondered the road ahead and unforeseen difficulties, which seemed dotted with invisible snares. "What have you devised with my father, as I know well of his disapproval?"

"As we discussed, I shall take you to London, because I would give you a season and so much more." When Henrietta shivered, Ernest frowned, unbuttoned his coat, pulled her closer, and tucked the folds about her. "However, Barrington and I shall introduce you as a distant cousin, several times removed, just arrived from the country."

"Thereby creating an acceptable history." Yet, she did not like the idea, because it was a lie. "And you believe that will satisfy the gossips?"

"It will if you play your part, because society respects strength. If you act as though you belong, it is doubtful they will question you." As he did when they were children, he toyed with her fleshy earlobe, and he heeled the stallion to a gallop. "But you will not be alone, so you need have no fear of discovery. Either Barrington, Florence, or I will be with you, at all times. Then, at the end of the Season, you and I shall wed. Where we go from there is no one's business."

"And if I choose not to marry you?" She held her breath, as he stiffened beneath her, because she had to consider the fact that his strategy might fail. "What will you do, Ernest?"

"I will let you go." Why did she not believe him? On the verge, a splendid landscape offered welcome distraction, as he drew rein, and she braced for his response. "Your father told me of his plans to send you to Paris, to open a boutique, and I pledged enough funds to finance the venture and purchase suitable living accommodations, until you can survive on your own. However, should you ever have need of me, I will assist you."

"You would do that for me?" Had she thought she loved Ernest? "You would forgo any protest?"

"Even if it kills me, and it might." She was not sure about that, but she was in no position to press for more, so she had to trust him. Holding her firmly in his grip, he teased her with his nose, and they shared another sweet kiss, which she was reluctant to end. "But I ask you to give us a chance at the happiness we coveted as children, because our dream is not so farfetched. Let us renew our acquaintance, although I submit it is wholly unnecessary, as you and I are so in tune as to render verbal communication gratuitous, despite the fact that our parents did their damnedest to separate us." He tucked a tendril behind her ear. "Yet, in so many ways, it is as if you never left Derbyshire."

"I know, as I feel the same." While so much of the man had grown and matured, his blue eyes remained constant, and it was there she found comfort and reassurance. In his gaze, she could journey through time, to the past, and to their youthful days, when they functioned as a single entity. She brushed his brown hair from his forehead and smiled. "And that is why I accept your proposal and commit fully to your plan."

CHAPTER FIVE

The streets of Chesterfield were alive with activity, as Ernest escorted Henrietta to the market. Wearing one of his best coats and a new pair of buckskin breeches, with his Hessians polished to a mirror-shine, he simmered with excitement, smiled, and acknowledged various locals of note, offering little in the way of information regarding the mysterious lady at his side. Brimming with pride, given the beauty on his arm, he resolved to purchase the entire lot of ladies' accouterments, if only to please Hen, because she accepted him, and it had been a long time since he savored the rousing taste of hope.

"Are you sure this is a good idea?" Fussing with the velvet bow of the dark green poke bonnet she borrowed from Florence, Henrietta bit her bottom lip. "And should I not have a chaperone?"

"Perhaps, but we will not let that stop us from enjoying ourselves, will we?" Indeed, nothing could temper the thrill of victory, as he embarked on the courtship to end all courtships. "And this is a most excellent idea, because I would have the world know you are mine."

"Are you not putting the cart before the horse?" She glanced at the two footmen, in tow. "We have made no announcement, and we have yet to survive the Season."

"A mere formality." Nothing could spoil the moment, as Ernest led her to a stall that featured a huge collection of hair adornments, because countless times he had envisioned indulging her. "Shall we begin here?" He selected a lovely silk bandeau. "What about this? Could you not use it to complete one of your unique ensembles?"

"What a stunning shade of red." Wrinkling her nose, she leaned close. "But the gathers are uneven, and there is no velvet underside to hold the bandeau in place. Without the velvet, the decoration will slip free."

"Well, let us continue, my dear."

A half an hour later, after perusing the entire collection, as if they were running a race at the Royal Ascot, they departed without buying a thing, because nothing met her standards. Hoping to have more luck with gowns, he ushered her into one of the town's most exclusive boutiques. Soon, he perceived no one could satisfy Henrietta's impeccable taste and unmatched requirements.

"Will nothing suit?" Disappointed, he ignored the nagging sense of failure that crept into his brain, spreading like some foul disease and gnawing at his flagging confidence.

"The dress is charming, but it is representative of last year's fashions and evidences no real talent for design." As she scrutinized a partially completed garment, she narrowed her stare and shook her head. "Look." She pointed for emphasis. "The hem is uneven, the side seams are crooked, and the heavy taffeta does not compliment but rather overwhelms the lighter tulle, when pairing textiles should be an elementary aspect of the planning phase. Does no one take pride in what they produce?" With a tsk, she returned the lackluster garment to the wall peg. "Such a pity, as the overall concept shows promise."

At the second store, she rejected the inventory of choices. When the third shop produced similar results, Ernest paused on the street corner.

"My dear, you may have to lower your expectations just a tad, as I cannot take you to the balls garbed in naught but your chemise and garters, although you would certainly attract attention." Then he seized upon a perfect solution. "What say we tour the mercantile, and you can select your own materials?"

"What a wonderful notion, because then I could sew my own clothes, which I prefer." In that moment, she bounced on her heels and favored him with a glowing smile, which cut through the chill and warmed him from top to toe. "And I should be inspired by the difference in inventory, as compared to Kent."

"Would that please you?" How he ached to kiss her, to take her in his arms and make love to her, if only to capture a small taste of her joy, her fire, and her spirit, because he could not remember a time when he enjoyed such unshakable certainty in his future. "Because I do wish to please you."

"My lord, you please me without even trying, and you always have, but you know that." She was correct in her assertion, because no one believed in him like Henrietta. Clicking her heels, she saluted, as she often did when they were young. "Lead, and I shall follow you anywhere."

That was their call to arms.

"I like the sound of that." Just as when they were children, in her adoring gaze he believed he could topple corrupt governments, defeat a slew of villains, and succeed in any noble endeavor with which she charged him, because she made him believe in himself. She validated him. She made him understand that he possessed a measure of self-worth. That he was more than just a sand-filled bag to be pummeled by his father.

That was why he lied to her.

That was why he could never let her go.

With an exaggerated bow, he chuckled and ushered her to the textile merchant.

As she examined bolt upon bolt of fabric, voicing approval of some while rejecting others, he remained in her wake, admiring her ability to negotiate prices. Indeed, she evidenced the same confidence that drew him to her, when he was but a green lad.

In some respects, between the two of them, she remained the confident, stronger partner. No matter the predicament, Henrietta always portrayed fierce conviction in her actions, and he often thought of her, as he mimicked the same mettle during various business deals, throughout his adult life, which carried him to victory. Yet, Ernest kept the truth hidden deep in his soul.

He was a fake.

He was a fraud, because he remained very much a prisoner of his father's abuse.

Upon her return, he became conscious of the fact he had been adrift as a ship without an anchor, after his father sent Hen to Kent. That was why he rarely ventured to Derbyshire. Everywhere he turned, he was reminded of the stablemaster's daughter, and the agonizing torment driven by her absence threatened to destroy him, as in her absence he lost her, again and again.

So many times, he had been tempted to travel to Kent. To find his ladylove. To bring her back to Garring Manor, but one thing kept him at bay. The fear that she found happiness without him. If he wandered the earth like a lost and wounded animal, the knowledge that she persisted in some sense of contentment would have struck the final blow.

"My lord, you woolgather." As he blinked, she nudged him in the ribs. "And in some respects, I do the same thing."

"Yes, you do." When he noted the pile of selections, he chuckled. In the end, it seemed he at last succeeded, although not as anticipated. "And it appears you do very well, my dear, given you have amassed a veritable mountain in materials."

"If it is too much, I can put some back." The glow in her cherubic cheeks ebbed ever so slightly, and he cursed his blasted hide. "Really, I do not need them all."

"You will do no such thing." As he caressed a swath of rich blue velvet, something occurred to him, and he eyed the shopkeeper. "We will take the entire lot, and I shall dispatch my footmen to retrieve the parcels. You may send the bill to Garring Manor, care of Lord Ernest Howe."

"Of course, my lord." The stodgy merchant dipped his chin.

"How does it feel to do that?" she asked, as they stepped onto the sidewalk.

"Do—what?" He waved to the footmen. "Collect my purchases and convey them to the coach."

"Aye, sir." The servants bowed in unison.

"What is it like to buy anything you want, whenever you want, without fear of going hungry or ending up in debtor's prison?" She settled her palm in the crook of his elbow, and he steered toward the next destination. "Because I am accustomed to counting every shilling."

"You will know, soon enough." Four doors down, he paused, turned the knob, and handed her over the threshold. "Once we are married, you will never again quibble over a few pounds."

"My lord, I do not want you for your money, and we just spent a vast deal more than a few pounds." As her shimmer faded, he understood he insulted her. "I would be happy if we never journeyed to London, and I spent my days in naught but my simple morning dresses."

"I apologize, Hen." He snapped his fingers, and the jeweler came alert. "I should not have insinuated your reasons for accepting my proposal were anything less than honorable, and my motives for enacting my plan are simple. I mean to marry you, and I will have you by my side, thereafter. In order for that to happen, we must introduce you to society, where you will accompany me to the various engagements I am required to attend. That has always been my dream, and now that we are reunited I will have it. And I will let nothing and no one stand in my way. Perhaps, I can make it up to you with something that sparkles."

"Ernest, where have you brought me and to what purpose?" She glanced left and then right, perused the displays of precious baubles, and flinched. "You cannot be serious."

"Ah, but I am determined to spoil you, my dear. In some ways, I have lived my whole life for this moment, and I shall have it. Please, indulge me, Hen." With his arm at her waist, he pushed her forward. "Good afternoon, Mr. Leighton."

"Lord Ernest, as always, it is a pleasure to see you." It struck Ernest, in that instant, that he bought several items from the purveyor of precious gems, over the years, for his ladybirds, and he did not want Henrietta confused as such, given the manner in which the jeweler gaped at her. "What can I show you? A bracelet, perhaps?"

"No." Indeed, that particular accessory often accompanied a farewell, and Ernest opted for the unvarnished truth of the situation, as Mr. Leighton did not travel in the same social circles. "I would like to show Miss Graham an assortment of betrothal rings, as well as a strand of pearls." The thrill of triumph almost moved him to tears, as he uttered the singular proclamation, because it brought him one step closer to the reality he coveted. "And if you have something to compliment a gown of blue velvet, I should like to see it."

"Ernest, what are you doing?" At his side, Henrietta dug her fingernails into his coat sleeve, but he pretended not to notice.

"I have just the thing." From a cabinet, Mr. Leighton drew a small box. Inside, on a bed of black satin, sat a variety of gold bands. "Let us begin with the foundation of the ring, and then we can pair it with a stone of your choice. If you will have a seat, Lord Ernest and Miss Graham."

"Excellent." Ernest held her chair until she was comfortably situated. Well, as comfortable as possible, under the circumstances. "Have you any preferences, Henrietta?"

"No, I do not." As she gazed on the selection, she bit her bottom lip and furrowed her brow. In unveiled agitation, she shifted her weight. Then she toyed with the hem of her sleeve. "I would be happy with a piece of string."

"I know you would." Grasping her wrist, he kissed her gloved knuckles. "And that is why you will have a diamond and anything else your heart desires."

"This understated but elegant band of polished gold would look wonderful on Miss Graham's slender fingers." Mr. Leighton held up the ring. "And you can pair it with a large, round-cut stone, if Miss Graham will remove her gloves, that I might take her size."

After much hesitation, and in some instances downright refusal to answer, Hen finally agreed on a simple, unembellished band with a one-carat diamond. Then Ernest picked a charming strand of pearls, which he insisted she wear. When the jeweler asked them to wait, as he collected something special from the back of the store, she leaned toward Ernest.

"My lord, this is too much." Toying with the necklace at her throat, she compressed her lips and then sighed. "How can I ever repay you for such extravagant gifts?"

"Sweetheart, it is my duty, as your husband, to dress and adorn you, thus there is naught to repay. But, if you insist, I am sure we can come to some agreement and a means of compensation that benefits us, both." When she made to protest, he silenced her with an upraised hand. "I beg you, indulge me, please. I have waited my whole life to do this, I am enjoying myself, immensely, and I wish to savor our day." After she nodded, he cupped her chin and winked. "Shall we continue?"

"All right." Her expression did not inspire confidence. "But take pity on me, and do not buy anything too expensive, as I am already overwhelmed by your generosity."

"Now then, as I was saying, I have just the item you require, Lord Ernest." Mr. Leighton set a large box on the table and lifted the lid, revealing an exquisite parure of sapphires and diamonds nestled in a bed of pure white satin. "This is an exclusive design created by one of my master jewelers, and the construction is unique to my shop. I guarantee there is nothing else like it in England."

Fashioned of gold, the baubles featured a gothic motif, with a combination of diamond scrollwork and leaf work and sapphire and pearl rosette-like mosaics comprising the necklace, bracelet, ring, two perfectly matched shoulder brooches, a larger single brooch, and earrings. Without doubt, the *pièce de résistance* was a tiara that boasted seven sapphire pinnacles, of which the middle one was the largest, and it impressed even Ernest in its splendor.

"Magnificent." He caressed a glittering gem. "We will take it."

"Ernest—*no*." Henrietta yanked on his arm, but he paid no heed. "If the other things were too much, that collection is beyond the pale, and I will not wear it."

"Yes, you will, and it will pale in

comparison to your beauty." To Mr. Leighton, Ernest said, "I will send my footman to fetch my purchases."

"As always, it is a pleasure doing business with you, my lord." The jeweler bowed. "And permit me to congratulate you on your engagement."

"Ernest Cornelius Frederick Howe, no matter what you say, I will not accept such an expensive gift, however well intended." In a familiar affectation that brought a smile to his face, because he could read her like a book, she thrust her chin and folded her arms, as he all but dragged her outside. "My lord, I have reached the end of my tether, and I wish to go home, because it is not appropriate for a woman of character, regardless of low birth, to accept such gifts, and I will not disgrace my father, as he taught me better."

"What a noble argument you make. Did he also teach you to obey your future husband?" Yes, he purposely taunted his lady, because he reveled in her company. "Else you could have difficulty sitting, during our married life, because I rather fancy the thought of spanking your bare bottom, though I would never hurt you."

"You would not dare." Her brown eyes flared. "And the operative word, which you conveniently omit, is *future*. You are not yet my lord and master, and at this rate you may never be, thus I retain my right to protest. I am not a child."

"Then do not behave as one." Tucking her hand in the crook of his elbow, he winked. "If you are to play your part, you must dress the part, and I plan to outfit you in a wardrobe fit for a queen, because you are my queen."

"Lord Ernest, this is an unexpected surprise." It was then he noticed Mrs. Dudley, the biggest gossipmonger in Derbyshire, as she wrinkled her nose and leveled her gaze on Henrietta. "And who is this young lady availing herself of such an estimable escort and one of the most eligible bachelors in England?"

He cursed under his breath.

"Mrs. Dudley, what a pleasure." With a nod of his head, he acknowledged the notorious busybody's presence, and at his side Hen stiffened. "Allow me to introduce Miss Henrietta Graham. While we would love to chat, Miss Graham and I are due at Garring, and we are already late, so we bid you a fond farewell."

With that, he drew Henrietta across the street and steered her toward the narrow medieval streets known as the Shambles and the Royal Oak pub.

"Are we in trouble?" When he spied fear in her usually charming countenance, he ducked into a cramped alleyway.

In the dim corridor, free of interlopers, he pushed her against a wall and did what he ached to do all afternoon. He kissed her.

Lush and ripe as a decadent strawberry, her lips posed a succulent temptation, and he deepened the connection, plunging his tongue into the warmth of her mouth, and she moaned. Fire scorched a path from their point of contact to the lethal part of his anatomy, which roared to life beneath his expensive, tailored garments, and never had Ernest felt more a man, as she shivered in his arms.

Teetering on the edge of some imaginary brink, he longed to take her, to hike her skirts, set her on her back, lift her heels, and lose himself in her most tantalizing flesh. Instead, he broke free and withdrew from his lady.

"Did I do something wrong?" She frowned.

"I wish you would not always presume the fault lies with you, when I am to blame for our inappropriate tryst, but I submit I am helpless to resist the lure you present, because

I desire you." Somehow, he just stopped himself from reengaging in behavior unbecoming a gentleman, as he offered his escort. "Now, let us share a meal and conversation, as we must strategize our next move, and I am sorely in need of a drink."

"And that would be—what?" Again, she rested her hand in the crook of his elbow and squeezed his arm. "I thought you planned to introduce me as a distant relation."

"Indeed." But the *ton* would not settle for something so pedestrian, and even the most plausible tale could prove unconvincing to the nosiest marriage-minded mama. "Yet, we must have care and create a new narrative, and one that omits any mention of your true history, if we are to succeed in our ruse." If only he could muster sufficient confidence to quiet his nagging doubts and bolster his fortitude, because theirs was tricky business. "In a sense, you shall be reborn."

~

In a sense, you shall be reborn.

As Henrietta sat in the back parlor, she gazed out the window and reflected on Ernest's declaration, which left much unsettled in her mind, because everything relied on her ability to deny her heritage, in the face of society's scrutiny. While he made it sound so simple to conceal the truth of her birth, she was not half so encouraged, because she could not escape the feeling that she was somehow betraying her father and her mother's memory, and she knew not how to be anything more than a stablemaster's daughter.

"May I join you?" In the doorway, Florence stood and smiled. "You appeared lost in thought, such that I was hesitant to disturb you."

"Oh, Flo, you could never disturb me." Henrietta leaped from the *chaise* and ran to embrace her childhood chum. Would that everyone in society could be so accommodating as her old friends. "And it is good to see you, as I need an ally right now."

"So I gather, after Ernest's impromptu shopping trip, which I suspect has left you out of sorts, given his lavish taste and generosity, where you are concerned." Flo ushered Hen to the sofa, and they relaxed. "And Barrington is furious, because he believes his brother does not guard your reputation, and I gather he intends to have words with Ernest." She clasped Hen's hand, twined their fingers, and gave a gentle squeeze. "While I have no desire to personally witness the exchange, I would dearly love to be a fly on the wall, and I fear we may be in for a bumpy courtship."

"But I do not wish to be the source of strife between them, as their relationship has always been a tad rocky." And such rancor did not bode well for Henrietta's fledgling union with Ernest, which already boasted plenty of complications, none of which inspired courage or conviction. "While I comprehend the need for secrecy, regarding my low background, I do not understand the urgency." She looked to Florence for advice. "Why can Ernest and I not simply elope? Why must we journey to London, and why must I enter society?"

"Because his social standing requires more of his bride. If you accept him, then you must also accept your place in his world." Flo sighed and shook her head. "Never was that impressed upon me so greatly until Barrington fled England, and I was forced to confront the responsibilities of my own stature, as I was expected to wed, because it was the thing to do, regardless of my emotional attachments. Given the contract negotiated by my father, I was bound to the marquessate, despite my objections."

"Which sounds so silly." Even as Hen voiced the comment, she discerned she would be expected to abide by the same ridiculous, unwritten rules, once she married Ernest. "I know little of etiquette, and I am to learn a new narrative, one that better suits the *ton*, but I am not sure that suits me."

"I can help with the dictates that govern our set, and I sympathize with your situation, as my father tried to persuade me to wed Ernest, regardless of my love for Barrington, and I refused to do so. Thus I found myself isolated from those who might offer support." Florence bowed her head and sniffed. "It was the darkest, loneliest time of my life, and the only thing that sustained me was the unshakeable belief that my man would return for me."

"And he did." Just as Henrietta returned for Ernest, and the similarities in their predicament was not lost on her. Did Ernest need Henrietta as Florence needed Barrington? "I can only hope I fare half so well as you."

A knock at the door cut short the conversation, and Flo stiffened her spine. "Come."

"I beg your pardon, my lady." Crawford bowed. "But a Mrs. Dudley and a Miss Dudley just arrived to pay call."

"Oh, no." Hen flinched. "Ernest and I ran into them, in Chesterfield. What could they possibly want?"

"It is all right. Let us not panic." Florence stood and smoothed her skirts. "Crawford, we will take tea and scones, in the drawing room."

"Again, I beg your pardon, my lady." The butler shuffled his feet. "But Mrs. Dudley expressed a desire to visit Miss Graham."

"No, I cannot do it." Hen wrung her fingers, as her knees buckled. "It is too soon. I know not what to say or how to act. Send them away, as I am not prepared to receive callers."

"We cannot do that without rousing suspicion, and Mrs. Dudley is the worst scandalmonger in England." Florence hugged her belly and humphed. "If we do not accommodate her, she will have you infected with the plague, increasing with Ernest's love child, and declare you the illegitimate daughter of Bonaparte, and the news would spread halfway across the county before the day is done."

"She would not dare." Angry in an instant, Hen clenched her fists. "She could not be so cruel, when I have done naught to her."

"Trust me, she has done much worse to complete strangers and reveled in their destruction." Lingering before a wall mirror,

Florence assessed her appearance and then glanced at Henrietta, and a chill of unease shivered down her spine. "Let us face the enemy, as a united front, and you will follow my lead."

"I do not have a good feeling about this." Henrietta bit her lip and wanted to vomit. "In fact, I am terrified by the prospect."

"Posh." Florence ushered Hen into the hallway. "Actually, I think it could be quite fun, if we take the right tack."

"I do not follow." As they neared the drawing room, her ears rang, and her heart hammered in her chest. "Whatever happens, I beg you, do not leave me."

"Chin up, dear friend." Florence gave Henrietta a playful nudge. "Let us do unto the Dudleys as they would do unto us, and enjoy a bit of sport at their expense."

"How I envy your spirit." Henrietta gulped, as she doubted everything about the impending meeting. "I think I am going to swoon."

"Smile, and you will do no such thing." Florence winked and swept into the elegant chamber. "Agnes, darling, how wonderful to see you, and you brought your charming daughter Druscilla with you, thus I am doubly blessed, today. To what do I owe this pleasant surprise?"

Henrietta almost choked on Florence's falsehood.

"Lady Ravenwood." Wide-eyed and sputtering, Agnes curtseyed. When she noted Druscilla remained stock-still, the mother snapped her fingers, and the daughter made her less than graceful obeisance. "I am so sorry to disturb you, given your condition, and I thought your butler understood I called upon Miss Graham."

"But Miss Graham is my honored guest." As a queen assumed her throne, Florence eased to a large, overstuffed chair. "Would you snub me in my own home?"

"Of course not, and that was not my intent, Lady Ravenwood." The gossipmonger blanched, and Henrietta barely suppressed a snort of laughter. "Forgive me for the confusion, as I would never be so impudent as to offend a noble of your estimable stature, but I had thought to welcome Miss Graham to our little community, as I presume she has few acquaintances and could, therefore, benefit from new friendships. Especially from a colleague of discrimination and breeding."

Ridiculous, insufferable woman.

"My, but you are the soul of charity."

Henrietta stifled a gurgle of laughter, as Crawford rolled the tea trolley into the room. Flo gazed at Hen, and she pondered her friend's scheme. "Would you be so kind as to pour, Henrietta?"

"Of course." Curious, she nodded. "It would be my pleasure."

As she fulfilled her charge, she studied Florence, as the marchioness engaged the interlopers in casual conversation, with skill and ease Hen could only admire. When she passed out the refreshments, Mrs. Dudley arched a brow.

"Must confess I adore your gown, Miss Graham. It really is remarkable, and I should commission a new wardrobe for my daughter, prior to our annual trip to London, for the Season, you know." Mrs. Dudley stared down her nose and assessed Hen from top to toe. "Did you purchase it at a boutique in London or Chesterfield, because I would love to know the designer?"

Unsure how to respond, Hen swallowed hard, because the dress was of her own making, and there was nothing like it in the immediate area. Then an idea came to mind. "I bought it at a little shop in Kent, but the store is no more, because the owner has since passed away."

"How unfortunate." The nosy woman snapped to attention. "So you hail from Kent?"

"Er—yes." Was that not the narrative Ernest suggested? Henrietta bit her tongue and glanced at Flo for guidance.

"What a coincidence." With a cat-that-ate-the-canary grin, Mrs. Dudley lowered her chin. "My mother was born in Kent, and her family still resides there. Perhaps you know the Blands of Tunbridge Wells?"

The world seemed to turn on its end.

"I do not believe so." Fighting panic and the urge to flee, Henrietta perched in a Hepplewhite chair near the window and rested her hands in her lap, because she only had to fool the intruders long enough for Flo to enact her hastily sketched plan. "But Kent is a rather large county, and I am but one person."

"What of your kin?" Druscilla, quiet until that instant, entered the fray, snatched a piece of shortbread from the tray, and shoved the confection none too delicately into her mouth. Then she mumbled, "Where were you born?"

Silence fell on the chamber.

In that instant, Florence sneezed.

"Oh, dear." The marchioness pressed a

111

palm to her cheek. "But I am chilled, and that is not good for a lady in my delicate condition."

"Shall I fetch your shawl?" Henrietta inquired.

"You are too kind to me." Florence smiled. "What would I do without you?"

"I am sure you would manage." As she strolled into the foyer, Hen rolled her shoulders, hiked her skirts, and ran upstairs. On the second-floor, she located Flo's lady's maid. "Mead, Lady Ravenwood requires her shawl."

"Right away, Miss Graham." The servant curtseyed and rushed toward the master suite. A few minutes later, she returned. "Shall I take it to her?"

"I can do that." Hen collected the knitted wrap. "Thank you."

"Yes, ma'am." Again, the maid made her obedience, which still disconcerted Henrietta, because she was one of them.

Upon returning to the landing, she noted Florence standing in the foyer, as she held open the door for Mrs. Dudley and Druscilla, and Henrietta ducked into the hall. Peering past the edge of the wall, she hid in the shadows and waited until Florence ushered the Dudleys across the threshold.

At last, the marchioness waved and then turned around. "You can come out now, as they are gone."

"Thank heavens." Heaving a sigh of relief, Henrietta charged the stairs and descended to the first floor. "How did you get rid of them so quickly?"

"I told them I felt faint, which is not necessarily untrue, given their odious company and my condition. Had they dawdled much longer, I might have been ill, in truth, and I wager they would not have enjoyed that." With a sly smile, Florence patted her belly. "But their encroachment is most unfortunate, because Mrs. Dudley views you as competition for her daughter, and I gather Ernest will not be pleased by the inauspicious development."

"What inauspicious development?" As if on cue, Ernest strolled into the foyer, from the general direction of the study, with the marquess at the rear, and he immediately settled his gaze on Henrietta. "Did something happen?"

Before Hen could respond, Barrington pulled his wife into his arms and gave her a vast deal more than thorough kiss, which brought the burn of a blush to Henrietta's cheeks, and she wished Ernest welcomed her in similar fashion. Not because she coveted the estimable nobleman, but because she longed for such reassurance from her beau. Could he not see the toll his plan exacted on her? Did he not understand that she died a little, every time she lied and denied her heritage?

"That awful Mrs. Dudley and her horrible daughter paid call, and they posed numerous questions about my background, for which I was unready to answer." Hen bit her bottom lip, as she prepared to deliver the ill tidings. "In my nervous state, I admitted I came from Kent, and Mrs. Dudley informed me that she has relations in Tunbridge Wells. Do you realize what that means?"

"You did *what?*" With hands on hips, Ernest shifted his weight, and she gulped. "I warned you were not to share any details regarding your personal history until we devised a proper story, because our narratives must match. Indeed, we must be as one, else our endeavor is doomed to failure. Would you undermine our efforts from the start? Really, Hen, how could you be so careless?"

"Yes, I know, and I apologize, but it was not my fault." To her chagrin, tears formed, because she had never been the target of Ernest's indignation, and she shuffled her slippered feet, in discomfit. "Can you not understand that I was anxious, and I knew not how to answer the woman without rousing suspicion?"

"So instead, you revealed the truth, which could threaten our entire enterprise and future, because Mrs. Dudley has ties to Tunbridge Wells." He sighed in unveiled frustration, and Henrietta wanted to crawl back to her father's cottage, but that was not an option for her. Given the disagreement, she had no choice or escape. "Do you want us to fail? Are you not in favor of our scheme and what we hope to achieve?"

"It could not be helped." She splayed her arms in entreaty. Could he not sense her distress? "Please, Ernest, I am sorry." To her shock and embarrassment, he dismissed her without so much as a dip of his chin and skipped upstairs. Stock-still, and her mouth agape, she stared at Barrington and Florence. "Truly, I meant no harm, but I know not how to be something I am not."

"It is all right, Hen, as it is not your fault my sibling seems to have forgotten his manners." Barrington gently set aside his bride and frowned. "But I believe it is past due for me to have a word with him, in your defense." He claimed another kiss from

Florence.   "Please, excuse me, darling, because it appears I must beat some sense into my little brother."

"Give him an extra swift kick in the arse, for compassion."   Flo giggled, but she sobered when she met Henrietta's gaze.   "In the meantime, what say you and I return to the drawing room and enjoy our refreshments?"

"I am not sure I can do this.   As of this moment, I am not even sure we can succeed." Adrift on a sea of indecision, Henrietta grasped Florence's hand and shook her head. "I love Ernest, and I always have, but I am not sure I can give him what he wants, as I know not how to be anything other than what I am—a stablemaster's daughter."

CHAPTER SIX

Late the following morning, Ernest turned up his nose at the untouched breakfast on the tray, stood, and strolled to the windows overlooking the garden. After a night spent tossing and turning, his mood had improved little since Henrietta's unfortunate revelation, because he could devise no way to mitigate her admission to the Dudleys.

While he would happily marry Hen in the stables, with naught but horses in attendance, his position in one of England's most estimable noble families required he observe the proprieties associated with his station, and he would do anything to protect his future wife, even if it meant surrendering his character and her personal history.

He was that desperate.

"Brother, you have avoided me long

enough, and I will not be ignored." When Ernest glanced over his shoulder, he discovered Barrington, looming in the middle of the sitting room. In his grasp, he clutched a large bundle of what appeared to be envelopes. "I must admit I never fully comprehended the depth of your attachment to Henrietta, and how much it mirrored my own for Florence, until now. I honestly thought it a child's fancy, but I know it is much more, so in some respects I owe you an apology." He handed Ernest the parcel. "When you told me of the letters Hen claimed she wrote, I remembered our father collected all of his correspondence, and I searched the heap and located her unopened missives, hidden among the stores."

"You found them?" With trembling fingers, Ernest reached for the treasured mementos. After untying the twine that bound them, he flipped through the franked dispatches, marked from Tunbridge Wells, Kent. As tears welled in his eyes, he hugged the notes to his chest and shook his head. "So she did not forget me, and I was never alone, as I imagined."

"How could she forget the love of her life?" Barrington rested a palm to Ernest's shoulder. "The simple answer is she could not, any more than Florence could forget me, because women possess incomparable strength and devotion, and that is doubly so when it comes to their heart. And I spoke with Graham, regarding your letters to Henrietta, and he has the entire lot, which she has never seen. It would appear our father franked but never posted them for you. Instead, he compiled the collection and sent them to our stablemaster, with instructions to burn them."

"So she bore the same excruciating silence, believing, however wrongly, that I needed her not. And I, so ignorant in my assumptions, doubted the constancy of her affection, when I heard nothing from her, because I presumed my entreaties fell on deaf ears." Ashamed, Ernest wiped his cheeks and gazed at the floor. "It was easier to assume she erased me from her memory, than to suspect, even for a second, she suffered the same agony and emptiness of our separation."

"I sympathize." Barrington eased to a high-backed chair, rested elbows to knees, and propped his chin in his hands. "Florence and I endured only five years apart, whereas you and Hen tolerated twice the estrangement, yet you remain joined at the hip, owing to your love, so I am confused by your tack and your treatment of her."

"I beg your pardon?" Ernest set the letters on a table and faced his irritating elder sibling. "If there is any chance for Hen to survive in society, we must redefine her. We must remake her into something more acceptable, else the *ton* will destroy her, and I shall be moved to violence if that happens."

"Are you sure about that?" In an annoying affectation, Barrington inclined his head and arched a brow. "Because our friends will never abandon us, which we learned when I returned to London as a wanted pirate. While there will always be those who shun you, what do they matter, when they are nothing to us?"

"They matter, because I want to give Hen everything. Power, prestige, and money. I would make her a lady, that she spends no more days with her nose pressed to the glass, watching our world from the outside, as a beggar, because she belongs with me. It is my dream, and I will have her by my side." Ernest would not allow the nobles to treat his bride-to-be with anything less than the respect that was due, when she far surpassed them in every way. "Once it is all said and done, and Henrietta and I are wed, she will understand why I acted as I did."

"And what of yesterday? What of her

dreams? Are you certain hers are aligned with yours?" Barrington just had to bring up the minor quarrel, when Ernest wanted to pay it no heed. "If anyone else treated Hen with such incivility, you would have challenged them to a duel, but you have yet to apologize, and she is hurt and confused by your behavior."

"I lost my temper, because I did not anticipate a visit from those meddling Dudleys, and I will make it up to her." He recalled her hurt expression and cursed himself, because he would rather sever an arm than injure his lady, thus he would make amends. "But she jeopardized everything, with her careless admission, as the Dudleys are trouble, and you know it."

"That is the point. Aside from Graham, Hen enjoys no close acquaintances in Derbyshire, and she is wholly unspoiled. In Kent, she was sheltered by her aunt and uncle, to her disadvantage, as she knows not how to dissemble, but I would argue that is a much sought after quality in a wife, so what happened was not her fault." Barrington scratched his chin and frowned. "You told me you met the Dudleys in Chesterfield, when you took Henrietta shopping, which was an exercise in lunacy, and I still cannot believe you were so reckless with her reputation. What did you think would be the outcome of the chance encounter? And what do you expect in London, because you cannot be everywhere at once? There will be occasions when Hen must feign for herself, sink or swim, and you will have to comfort her when she falls—and she will fall, as it is inevitable, which you would do well to admit."

"Not if I prepare her." Pondering various options, Ernest composed a script, of sorts, in his mind. And he would work with Hen, to ensure she made no mistakes, with none the wiser. They would create a catalogue of answers, from which she would not deviate, and they would win the day. Then they could retire to Derbyshire and begin their life, together. "And I will apologize for my odious behavior, but I was shocked by the unfavorable development, and you know my temper. But I want this, brother. For so long, I have wanted her, and she is within my grasp."

"Still, that is no excuse for rudeness, and you know better, especially when it comes to Henrietta." Barrington wagged a finger. "Hers is a gentle soul, and I will not permit you to mistreat her, however good your intentions. And another thing, you upset

Florence, and that I will not abide, under any circumstances, so you will make your apologies, else you will deal with me."

"What are you going to do, spank me?" Ernest took offense at his brother's interference. "Take the lash to my back? Or will you lock me in my room, without dinner?"

"I am not our father, and you would do well not to insult me, when I am on your side." Barrington compressed his lips. "But you must use care with Henrietta, and before you rip at me, I caution you not because I consider her low, as I would assert she is anything but low, but because she is my friend. Where she is concerned, I hold no illusions, and calling her naïve is putting it mildly. While Hen is not stupid, she is unfamiliar with the ways of the world and the dictates that govern our set, and you hurt her with your criticism, which she did not deserve. Do not abuse her again, because I will defend her, and you do not want to face me under those circumstances."

"I told you I would apologize." In that moment, Ernest checked his tone, because he needed an ally, thus he could ill-afford to alienate his brother. "What more would you have of me?"

"I would have you atone for your boorish behavior." Folding his arms, Barrington sat upright. "I would have you offer her a treat she has yet to sample and, in the process, spend some time with me, as I would mend our differences."

Curious, Ernest narrowed his stare. "What have you in mind?"

"I just purchased a pair of handsome bays, and I would like to have them put to, that I might try out their paces." Lowering his chin, Barrington smiled. "Care to race those pretty blacks of yours, with your future wife at your side?"

"Hen would love that." In seconds, Ernest assessed his appearance. "Give me a chance to change my coat, secure her forgiveness, and join you in the stable yard."

~

For the second time in as many minutes, Henrietta measured the length of a sleeve, before pinning the swath of wool to the top of the garment. Surrounded by various swatches, organized with precision, she scrutinized her fledgling creation and groaned. In a failed attempt to distract herself from the uncertainty of her situation, she designed, cut, and assembled a new gown, but she struggled to sew a single straight stitch, and she resolved to rip out the inferior work and redo the entire lot.

"May I come in?" When she glanced toward the door, she met Ernest's troubled stare, just as he stepped forward, and she winced. "Am I intruding, dearest and sweetest Henrietta?"

"You may suit yourself, sir, as this is your home." And never had she felt more unwelcome, since their heated exchange the previous afternoon. "I am just a visitor."

"I suppose I deserve that, after the shameful way I treated you, yesterday." Was that genuine remorse she detected in his words? "May a humble beggar grovel at your feet, that you might forgive his breach in proper decorum, given you are more than a visitor?"

"You require no permission to do as you please." As tears welled, she gave him her back, if only to spare her pride, because his caustic remarks still stung. "And you owe me nothing. Indeed, I should be able to fashion enough garments to repay you for the textiles. As for the jewels, I collected the entire lot on the vanity, and I hope you can return them. If you wish me to remove to my father's cottage, I can do so, at once, and continue my labors, there."

"Actually, I owe you everything, and you are going nowhere." When he rested his hands on her shoulders, she flinched. "I am so sorry I yelled at you, Henrietta. There is no excuse for my behavior, and I have no defense, except to say that I was wrong, pure and simple, and I cannot apologize enough."

"When the Dudleys arrived, I did not know how to respond, and I was unprepared to answer their questions. In truth, I wanted to avoid them, but Florence said that would only inspire gossip, which we could ill-afford, so I made the best of it." And she wondered just how much else she was not equipped to handle, in regard to his scheme. "I was only trying to help, and I never meant to undermine your plans."

"I know that." Gently, he rotated her and pulled her into his arms, and she did not resist. Instead, she nuzzled his chest and inhaled his sandalwood scent. "Please, Hen. I am your most humble servant, and I would rather cut off my most prized appendage than ever cause you pain, but my criticism was born of fear, because we are so close to achieving our dream. Can you not comprehend my reaction, with so much at stake? Can you not forgive me?"

"Yes, I forgive you, but I wonder if we

should rethink our future." He tensed, as she shifted to meet his gaze. "What if we reach for the impossible? What if we embark on a fool's errand, only to be destroyed in the end?"

"Would you surrender me so easily, because I would never sacrifice you without a fight." The anguish in his expression gave her pause. "What happened was entirely my fault, because I should have anticipated Agnes Dudley's attack, given her exploits are well known, from London to Derbyshire, and we would do well to guard against her. In any case, I am to blame, and I should not have yelled at you." He bent his head and claimed a whisper of a kiss. "But I am afraid, Hen. Now that you are back in my life, I am terrified of losing you. So, should I kneel? Should I prostrate myself at your feet and beg your forbearance?"

"That is not necessary." Beneath the weight of his contrition, her fit of pique vanished, but the pain remained, and she had serious reservations about his proposal. "I was thinking I could return to Papa's cottage, in any case, as I do not require a London season, and perhaps we could marry when you retire to Derbyshire for the summer."

"Frightened, my little bird?" How well he

read her thoughts, as he caressed her cheek.

"Yes." She nodded, as she cherished his dream. "Petrified."

"Please, do not worry, and let me give you a season, as a prelude to our nuptials, that you might persist in society as my bride." With his thumb, he toyed with her lower lip, until she caught him between her teeth. "Ah, but you tempt me, Henrietta, and I adore you. Trust me, I will not let you fall. Together, we shall compose a story and a collection of responses, so you will never again find yourself in a position of indecision or weakness. And I will remain firmly entrenched at your side, so there is no doubt as to the constancy of my affection and your place in my family."

"What if I do not want to go to London?" Given what she knew of the capital, she had no interest in venturing there. "I am a provincial, and I am proud of it. Is that not enough for you?"

"Sweetheart, do you not see? I am a man of wealth and position, and my wife must fulfill the duties expected of her, regardless of personal preference. That includes the annual trek to London, the journey through the ballrooms of the *ton*, dinner parties at home, and evenings at the opera, the theater, and

Vauxhall." Cupping her chin, he brought her gaze to his. "Would you have me take another, when my heart is set on you?"

"No." In fact, she gulped at the prospect. "The mere suggestion makes me want to be violently ill."

"Then give us a chance." Again, he claimed her lips in a scorching kiss. "Please, my little bird. Do it for those two children who dared to dream of something more and now stand in a position to claim the prize."

"You know I could never resist you or your charming pout." When he exaggerated his forlorn countenance, she laughed. "All right, we will do it your way."

"Wonderful." In a flash, he lifted her in his embrace and twirled her about the room. "Now, what say we take a ride in my phaeton? My brother wagers his new bays can outpace my blacks, but with you in my box seat, I cannot lose."

"It sounds like fun, but I should put on a warmer gown." In her mind, she sifted through a selection of options and decided on the lavender wool, with a matching pelisse and bonnet. "Give me five minutes, and I will meet you in the foyer."

"Do not make me wait too long." With a cat-savoring-cream grin, he let her slide down the front of him, and what should have been a harmless act struck her as quite illicit, thus she studied the floor, until he took her hand in his and nibbled on the tips of her fingers. "You are mine, Hen, just as I am yours. Regardless of what anyone says or what happens, never forget that."

"Yes, my lord." Once he exited her chamber, she raced to the armoire, located the lavender gown, laid it on the bed, and then initiated a strange tug of war with her laces.

It was in the solitude of her room that she reflected on her situation and what she was willing to surrender for Ernest. While she doubted not her ability to play the part of society lady, in public, she would still be naught but the stablemaster's daughter, in private. No matter how many stories her beau concocted, he could not recreate her, but she would wear the mask he contrived, because she loved him. But could they survive on love, when they lived so perilously on the edge of exposure? Would his attachment outlast her unveiling, if and when it happened?

CHAPTER SEVEN

"Yaa!" Ernest flicked the reins, and his team soared across the meadow, with Barrington just keeping pace. Holding tight, Henrietta squealed, as they rounded the curve, and when he let the blacks have their heads, his phaeton left Barrington in the dust. The pair charged forth, veering from left to right, and Ernest's heart pounded in his chest. By the time they reached the rise in the lane, which marked the end of the race, there was no question as to the winner, and Ernest beamed with pride.

"Oh, my lord, that was thrilling." Shifting, Hen momentarily rested her palm to his thigh, and his loins went up in flames, before she flinched and snatched free. With an arresting blush in her cheeks, she glanced toward the rear, as she clasped her hands in her lap, and he vowed, then and there, to maintain her breathtaking smile for the rest of their lives. "Apologies."

"Little bird, never apologize for touching me, because I belong to you." He leaned close and whispered, "How I look forward to the day you know me intimately."

"Ernest, stop." Despite her reproach, she grinned, and he could not resist baiting her. "You, sir, are a reprobate."

"Only with you, and do you not wish to know me?" As Barrington neared, Ernest winked. "Are you not curious?"

"You know I am." When she fixated on his mouth, he tensed. "And I—"

"Well, that was a miserable debut, and I am rather disappointed." Barrington pulled alongside, drew rein, and frowned, as he assessed the bays. "They need a bit of work, so enjoy your victory, however brief."

"I challenge you to a rematch, any time." Ah, it was as days of old, as Barrington taunted Ernest. "Perhaps, you would like to continue to the bluffs? You may have more luck."

"I need no luck, little brother." With a flick of his wrist, Barrington turned his team. "Now, I shall return to Garring and let my beautiful bride nurse my wounds, as she excels at her special brand of succor."

Waggling his brows, he offered a mock salute and then urged the bays into a trot. Alone with Henrietta, Ernest swooped, and she shrieked, as he hauled her into his lap and kissed her. As usual, he ignited the instant they touched.

Fire poured through his veins, pooled in the pit of his belly, traveled south, and he erupted. Unleashing the hunger he struggled to keep in check, he traveled a passionate path with his hands, inviting her to sample the fiery fruit of their shared ardor, and she did not disappoint him.

For several heated, groping, desperately intense minutes, he ravished his lady, and she resisted not, as she speared her fingers into his hair and teased his tongue with hers, until, at last, he ended their tryst, before he took her beneath the sky.

"I want you, sweet Henrietta." As she clung to the lapels of his hacking jacket, she inhaled a shivery breath, and he tightened his hold. "Such that I cannot trust myself to behave when I am near you."

"I understand, because I share your difficulty." With her nose, she traced the curve of his neck and then nipped his chin. "Are we bad? Is it wrong to feel this way?"

"For us?" Chuckling, he shuffled her in his grasp, and she sat upright. "No, sweetheart. I think it perfectly natural, given our longstanding attachment, as well as our separation. Now that we are reunited, I am anxious to prepare for our life, as a couple, and I wanted to discuss that."

"Oh?" She slid back to her seat and settled her pelisse and skirt.

"Barrington told me the Whitstone property is for sale, and I thought it would make a perfect summer home for us." Indeed, it was the next step in his plan to live the dream he cherished. Grasping the reins, he steered his horses toward the north end of the family estate. "It is relatively close, although it is small, by comparison with Garring, because it has only twenty-six bedchambers, but I suppose we can manage."

"Only twenty-six bedchambers?" She coughed. "Remember, I grew up in the stablemaster's cottage, which has but two private rooms, so I think it more than adequate, but I sincerely hope you do not expect me to clean such a large place."

"No, my dear." He snickered in the face of her naïve question, because it evidenced her provincial nature, which he adored. "Such services are beyond your new position as lady of the manor. Rather, you will need to interview and hire a small compliment of servants, and I have engaged my solicitor to compose a list of prospective homes in London, because we will maintain more than one residence. And I would also like to purchase something on the coast. Something isolated and remote, because I want you all to myself, once we are wed."

"I love the sound of that, but nothing too extravagant, please." With her arm wound about his, she rested against his shoulder, and he kissed the crown of her brown curls. "I am unaccustomed to such luxury, and I prefer a simple life."

That was part of the problem.

Once she married him, her life would be anything but simple, but it would have advantages.

Anxious to show his bride-to-be their future abode, he picked up the pace, and they sped past the vibrant countryside, until they approached a gated entry. After passing the brick-columned, wrought iron ingress, he slowed the team, just before they traversed a wide bend. The oaks parted to reveal a stunning view of the Palladian-styled home.

"You must be joking." Hen tensed and snapped to attention. "However you wish to describe it, that is a mansion."

"Nonsense, darling." He indulged in a bit of levity at her expense. "The somewhat modest residence boasts white stucco, three huge porticoes, a slate roof, six Corinthian columns, a wrought iron balcony at center, and a curved bay with massive windows. But my favorite feature is the balustraded parapet above the cornice of the entabultar, within which an attic story of three windows surmounts a lead saucer dome. Although it is not as large as Garring Manor, we should be able to accommodate approximately seventy guests, which is a lovely number for a summer party. Is it not marvelous?"

"It is certainly something." With a hand pressed to her throat, she blanched. "Ernest, are you serious about this?"

"Of course." Hers was not the reaction he anticipated, and his confidence waned. "Do you not like it?"

"On the contrary. It is the most beautiful thing I have ever seen." As she studied the structure, she reached for his hand and twined her fingers in his. "Never in my most ambitious dreams did I imagine living in such a grand house, and I know not what to say except to offer my thanks, which pale by comparison to what you offer."

"Say you will live with me, here. Say you will make it our home and fill it with our children. Say that I will find you in my bed, every night. Say I will wake to your countenance, every morning. Promise me that, which you once vowed as a girl, and nothing more, and I will set the world at your feet." In that instant, she came alert, and he chuckled. "It is just as we planned, when we were young, is it not? We shall be Barrington and Florence's neighbors, and we will raise our families, together. If your father is amenable, he can reside with us, or he can occupy one of the four smaller buildings, to the south. How does that sound? If you cannot be happy here, I can search for something else. Perhaps, something bigger."

"Oh, no." She laughed. "I would have been satisfied with a cottage similar to Papa's, but I suspect you prefer this, and I cannot complain."

"All right." Ernest slapped his thigh. "I shall instruct my solicitor to draw up the contract and purchase the estate." He slipped an arm about her shoulders. "And now I would seal our first milestone with a kiss."

Without further ado, he bent and covered her mouth with his.

~

The sun sat low on the horizon, as Ernest drove the phaeton into the stable yard, and a couple of attendants rushed to the fore. The notion that servants should wait on Henrietta still did not sit well with her, because she considered herself one of them, yet Ernest made it clear that marriage to him involved a transition, of sorts, in her identity, and she remained conflicted about what he believed was a natural progression in her status.

When her father appeared, she checked her attire, because her beau wreaked sweet havoc on her bodice, during their heated celebration, which tested the limits of her self-control, because no man had ever fondled her bare breasts, much less suckled her nipples, but she long ago decided she could deny him nothing. For the better part of an hour, they parked beneath the canopy of a mighty oak and engaged in salacious activity that seemed perfectly normal for a devoted couple in love, except he had yet to make his declaration. Still, she did not doubt him.

But she doubted everything else.

"Well, that was a rather stimulating ride." After disembarking, Ernest turned to hand her down, and his sly smile conveyed a wealth of meaning she understood too well. "You blush, my little bird. Dare I ask why?"

"You know the reason, sir." As her father neared, she lowered her voice. "And you are shameless."

"Where you are concerned, always." Ernest winked and then sobered. "Good evening, Graham."

"Will you be needing the phaeton, again, sir?" Papa glanced at her, and she averted her stare, because she was still angry with him. "Or shall I have it stored."

"You may park it, as I am in for the night." Ernest took her by the arm.

"Er—I wonder if I might have a word with Henrietta." At her father's query, she stiffened her spine, because she had nothing to say to him. "Please. It will only take a moment."

"Darling?" Ernest pressed his lips to her forehead. "You should honor your father's request, as to do otherwise is bad form."

"But I am angry with him." Conscious of those present, and unwilling to enact a scene, she whispered, "He betrayed us."

"Do it for me." Ernest cupped her chin. "I know you are upset, and I sympathize with your position, but we cannot begin our life based on a foundation of disagreement and conflict, and I would have his blessing, freely given."

"All right." As she regarded her father, she kicked a small stone. "What can I do for you, Papa?"

"Can we talk inside, as what I wish to discuss is of a personal nature, my dear?" Her father cast an expression of remorse, and her heart melted, because she needed to believe in him, yet he disappointed her. "I promise, it will not take long."

"Of course." With reluctance, she let go of Ernest and crossed the yard. As she ascended the entrance steps of the little cottage she once called home, she rued the quarrel that put her at odds with her father, given he was one of the two most important men in her life. "I do not have much time, because dinner will be served, soon, and I would not be late."

"Then I will not delay." At the tiny table at which he took his meals, he pulled out a chair. "Please, have a seat."

"What is this about, Papa?" In an instant, she swallowed hard and moderated her tone, because he taught her to respect her elders. "That is, what can I do for you?"

"It is what I can do for you that concerns me." For a moment, he just studied her, and she fidgeted beneath the weight of his perusal, as the situation grew awkward. Then he sighed. "First, I owe you an apology, because I hurt you, and that was never my intent."

"What did you think would happen when I found out you conspired with Lord Ravenwood to separate me from Ernest? Did you expect me to cheer your betrayal?" White-hot anger simmered beneath her skin, and she gritted her teeth, else she might lose her temper and say something she regretted. At last, she inhaled a deep, calming breath. "Regardless of my age, at the time, you knew what Ernest meant to me. Where was the harm?"

"As God is my witness, I thought it nothing more than a childhood fancy, which I believed you would outgrow." He rested his clasped hands atop the table and furrowed his brow. "I supposed you would forget him, as I assumed he forgot you, once you experienced life beyond these walls, and Lord Ernest was sent to Eton."

"How little you know me, because Ernest is my love. Despite eleven years apart, we remain united, as one, because I know him as well as I know myself." The pain of the past surfaced, cutting through her like the sharpest knife. "But you I do not know. You are a stranger to me, as I never presumed you could be so cruel."

"I am so sorry, Henrietta." Tears welled in his eyes, and he dragged his shirtsleeve across his face. "You have my word, I honestly believed I was doing the right thing, because I would do anything to protect you, and there were other factors that influenced my decision, of which you know not."

"Does it matter? When you should have championed me, instead, you broke my heart, because I always considered you my hero." Riding a wave of fury mixed with monumental disappointment, she refused to cry. "You, of all people, denounced me, and I know not how to trust you, anymore."

"And I wish I had never got involved, but it is too late to undo what is done." Shaking his head, he compressed his lips. "But I counted on the money to provide a secure future for you. In fact, I have spent none of it, as it is deposited into an account, which I have never touched. The funds are yours to do with as you see fit, and they offer you freedom. True liberation, not the gilded cage in which you now find yourself."

"I do not want your money, anymore than I want Ernest's, and I am not a prisoner, Papa. Rather, I have grasped the reins of destiny, and I ride for my dream." In a fit of temper, she pounded a fist. "All I ever wanted was to be loved, and you took me from the one person who promised to love me for the rest of his days."

"Henrietta Katherine, be reasonable." Papa exhaled. "You were but a child of eight—"

"With a woman's hopes and dreams." And it unnerved her that he discounted her feelings so casually. "We may have been young, but we knew what we wanted, and you schemed with Lord Ravenwood to destroy us. That is what I cannot comprehend, given your professed desire to protect me."

"Clearly, I made a mistake, because I did not fully grasp the lengths to which you were prepared to go, in order to secure your dream. I underestimated you, and I cannot apologize, enough. I know I hurt you and damaged your faith in me, and I will never forgive myself for that, but there is something I can do to atone." To her surprise, on the table he set a bundle, which he pushed in her direction. "These belong to you, but the late Lord Ravenwood gave them to me, for safekeeping, after he franked but never posted them for his son. I had thought to burn them, but for some reason I kept them. Perhaps, to give to you, now, and I pray they bring you some measure of comfort."

In silence, she untied the parcel, peeled back the swath of cotton, and discovered a cache of letters. As she flipped through the missives, she noted the marquess's franking, as well as the dates, and she emitted a soft sob of shock.

In the blink of an eye, she transformed to the girl of eight, that version of herself that believed in fairytales and knights in shining armor, frightened and alone, as she journeyed by coach to a strange place. Fear consumed her, as she clutched the wilting remnants of the last bouquet of cowslips Ernest gave her, until nothing remained but the memories, which faded with each passing day. But the agony entrenched deep in her soul, ever tormenting, relentless in its ability to wound her whenever she harkened to her childhood days at Garring Manor.

"Have you any idea of the pain you could have spared me, had you been honest with me? Do you know how I suffered, due to Ernest's apparent indifference, because he did not respond to my pleas for some sign of remembrance?" Leaping to her feet, she knocked over the chair, as she clutched the precious collection of envelopes to her chest. "I thought I meant nothing to him. I believed it a lie, and it crushed me. You brought me here to apologize, but you sink the knife deeper. I might have been able to forgive you for sending me to Kent, but this? In truth, I cannot abide to look at you."

"Henrietta, I admit I did not take the time to reflect on the effects my decision would have on you, but I had the best of intentions." Papa stood, and she averted her gaze. "And whether or not you wish to admit it, I was right about your status. The upper class will never accept you as their equal, because you are naught but a stablemaster's daughter."

"A fact of which you are so eager to remind me, Papa." In that instant, Henrietta pinned him with her stare and bared her teeth. "While I may not be to the manor born, you are the worst hypocrite. You criticize those who would define me as low, but you are the one who endeavored to keep me there. When you should have been my most vocal defender, as you are my father, instead you sided against me, and I am ashamed of you. Not because you are a servant, but because you discriminate against Ernest, based on his birth. You have become that which you protest."

With that, she turned on a heel and ran from the cottage, to her father's entreaties, but she ignored him. In search of solace, she sprinted across the yard and entered Garring through the terrace doors. When she burst into the hallway, she almost knocked down Ernest.

"Hen?" He held her at arm's length, as tears streamed her cheeks. "What is wrong, darling? What happened with your father?"

"He lied to me, Ernest." Clinging to the bundle of letters, she launched herself at her beau, as he represented everything noble and true in her world. "He lied about everything."

"Shh." Cradling her head, he held her tight. "It is all right, my little bird. What our fathers did is in the past, and it is better left there. What matters is that we are together, and nothing will keep us apart."

"I have your letters." She sniffed and shifted to look at her man. "I am so sorry I doubted you, when you told me you wrote to me. I thought you said what you wanted me to hear. I thought you forgot me."

"How could I forget my heart?" With his hands, he framed her face and pressed his lips to hers. Soothing warmth blossomed in the pit of her belly, unfurling and spreading throughout her limbs, erasing the pain and supplanting the misery with the promise of pleasure. When he mingled his tongue with hers, she moaned her appreciation, until he lifted his head. "And I have your correspondence, which Barrington located, hidden among my father's personal effects."

"Oh, let us read them, together." She bounced. "I am so anxious to know what you wrote, and I am even more excited for you to know what I pledged, over and over, during our separation, because we are a pair."

"What say I come to your sitting room, after dinner?" With a boyish grin, which tugged at her heart, he gave her a gentle squeeze. "As I am equally curious to know what you shared with me."

"My lord, it is a date."

CHAPTER EIGHT

The house was quiet, as Ernest hugged the wall and watched for any sign of servants, because he would not play fast and loose with Henrietta's reputation, and he could not allow anyone to see him entering her private chambers. As he tiptoed—yes, he bloody tiptoed down the corridor, he glanced over his shoulder. At last, he arrived at the door to her room, and he turned the knob, set wide the oak panel, and peered inside.

Light from the fireplace bathed the chamber in a soft saffron glow, and several tapers provided additional illumination. Sitting on a *chaise*, Hen glanced up, as he crossed the sitting room and joined her.

"My lord, I am uncontrollably excited." She smiled. "In fact, I did not think I could eat dinner, given I was so anxious to read your letters."

"I know the feeling." As he untied the bundle, he studied the similar collection nestled in her lap. "Must confess I have thought of nothing else, my little bird, since Barrington gave them to me, this afternoon."

"Shall we begin?" She poised with an envelope in her hands. "I arranged mine in order, based on when they were franked."

"After you." He delighted in her unmasked joy, as she tore open the missive, and he gave his attention to his assortment.

Opting to organize her letters by date, he ripped the edge of the very first correspondence she sent and plummeted into despair so palpable that his eyes welled. The anguish penned by a much younger Hen wrenched his heart, as she expressed the emptiness and pain in a child's terms.

Myriad vignettes sprang to life, animated visions of a girl's fancy depicted in precise detail, that he might persist in her world, even if only via the written word.

The second note detailed similar, extended agony, and her desperation shook him to his core, as she pleaded with him to write to her. The third and fourth exchanges buried him in hopelessness, while repeating her requests for some response from him, and that was the cruelest cut of all, because he endured the same torture.

Likewise, despite the separation, and independent of each other, they clung to the habits they once indulged, as she collected the cowslips he once brought her, harkening to her devoted beau. The sentimental gesture, raw in its desperation, brought him so very low.

It was then he became aware that Henrietta stared at him, holding one of his letters to her, and the tears streaming her cheeks mirrored his own.

"You missed me." She cast a tremulous smile. "And you wanted to visit me."

"Did you ever doubt me?" He unfolded another missive. "Because I longed to see you."

"I am ashamed to admit I did." As she fumbled with a handkerchief, he none-too-elegantly wiped his face. "Your silence struck a blow, because I did not know your father never posted your letters, and he kept mine from you. Oh, what we lost, Ernest. It is unbearable to contemplate."

"Were he alive, I would never speak to him again." The bitterness of hate filled his mouth, and he swallowed hard. "As it stands, I will never forgive him for taking you from me."

For a while, they simply sat there and stared, as unspoken passion simmered about them. There were so many things he wanted to tell her, so many sentiments he needed to share, yet he remained mute. Then the invisible dam burst, he reached for her, as she reached for him, and passion erupted as soon as they touched.

Amid the crackling parchment and missives that dropped to the floor, as autumn leaves scattered in the breeze, nothing could dampen their fervor. It was always the same, when their lips met. Soothing warmth pervaded his flesh, shivered along his spine, and settled as a comforting heat in his loins. Fire charged his nerves, consuming him in its intensity, and he gave himself to the raw hunger that burgeoned in his belly.

After loosening the bodice of her gown, he inched down the silk fabric, untied the ribbon of her chemise, and bared her beautiful breasts. With his tongue, he flicked her tempting nipples and then suckled from her delicate flesh, until she wiggled, moaned, and yanked his hair.

Riding a wave of lust, driven by so much pent up emotion; he lifted Henrietta from the *chaise* and carried her to the inner chamber, where he flung her atop the bed. In seconds, he covered her and gave her his weight. It was the first time he rested his hips to hers, and he pressed his rock-hard erection against her.

"Ernest, *please*." Her brown eyes flared in the wake of her appeal.

That was the one plea guaranteed to waylay his defenses, and all trace of rational thought fled him.

Shifting, he pulled up her skirts, eased between her creamy thighs, unhooked his breeches, freed his length, positioned himself, and thrust.

Thus, he claimed her, irrevocably.

There were precious moments in his life that he committed to memory, that such reveries might sustain him in his darkest hours, and they all centered on his lady. The first time he kissed Henrietta. The first time they held hands. The first time they pledged their undying love. The day he was told she departed Garring Manor. The afternoon she fell from the tree, into his lap, and into his world. But the instant in which they first joined their bodies in the most intimate connection known to humanity would reign supreme as the most treasured recollection of all.

Her cry of pain was enough to temper his movements, as he held perfectly still and framed her cheeks. It was then he discovered he seized her bride's prize, and that should not have surprised him, but it did. Focusing on her needs, as she whimpered, he kissed her, withdrew, and reseated himself fully within her.

"Shh, love." He repeated the decadent slip and slide, again and again. "Wrap your legs about me, sweetheart."

"Like this?" She furrowed her brow and held him in her sweet embrace, which enabled him to sink deeper inside her. "*Oh.*"

"Perfect, my little bird." Summoning the finesse honed in the company of some of the most experienced courtesans in London, he put Henrietta's needs before his own and slowed his pace, as completion beckoned, because he would wait for her release. In some sort of fiendish game, he increased and then moderated the rhythm, stroking her supple sheath, enticing her to yield herself to the pinnacle of their fiery coupling.

Of course, he should have known she would not make it easy on him, and she a proved a most demanding lover, testing his persistence and prowess. Desire swirled and soared, delivering him to heretofore-unimaginable heights of sensuality, and at some point he lost himself in the inferno, until she stiffened, dug her nails into his shoulders, and screamed.

On the heels of her healthy release, Ernest rose above her, gazed on his future wife, surrendered to the salacious storm, and the resulting completion carried him beyond anything he had ever experienced.

~

The candles had guttered, but a blaze still burned in the hearth, as Henrietta woke and stared at the canopy of her bed. For a few minutes, confusion reigned, as she remained unsure of her surroundings. Then a torrent of licentious images flooded her consciousness. Ernest kissing her. Touching her. Filling her. Myriad sensations coursed her skin, and passion blossomed anew. When she perceived her man sprawled atop her, with his flesh buried deeply—intimately in hers, she panicked and flinched.

In that instant, he opened his eyes, snuffled, gazed at her, and smiled, and she was not sure how to characterize his expression, when he waggled his brows. "Hello, my naughty little bird."

"You are one to talk." Of course, he was in a playful mood, when she needed her rational Ernest. "If memory serves, you are the one who initiated our tryst." As he stretched, he flexed his hips, and she sucked in a breath. "But I did not fight you."

"No, you did not, to my infinite gratitude, not that I expected you would." To her discomfit, he withdrew and pushed from the mattress, and she shivered in the absence of his warmth. To make the situation worse, if that was possible, his behavior did not inspire confidence, as he untied his cravat, yanked the yard-length of linen from his neck, and draped the swatch of cloth over the back of a chair. Soon, he doffed his coat and shirt. Then he sat to pull off his Hessians. Was he planning to stay? "By the by, why did you not tell me it was your first time?"

"What?" Never would she have predicted that query, and she scooted upright, more than a tad hurt by his slight. "How dare you say such a thing. Do you think so little of me?"

"My apologies, darling, as that must have sounded awful, when I intended no insult." When he stripped from his breeches, as though it were an everyday occurrence to disrobe in her presence, she studied the damask print of her counterpane. "Given your age, it would not have surprised me had you experimented with some lucky fellow in Kent, and it would have mattered not, because nothing could diminish my devotion to you. And you were so cooperative with me, in the north field, after our phaeton race with Barrington, that I assumed you had already experienced lovemaking. That you were untouched, and I claimed your most intimate gift, means more to me than you will ever know, and I am honored, my dear."

"Why would I ever deny you anything, least of all my body, when I have known you all my life? And you are the only man to know me thus. Have you known other women?" When he nodded, she frowned. "I am not sure how to feel about that."

"Sweetheart, society places different expectations on men, and my father purchased my first mistress for me, when I was but six and ten, and he left me no choice in the matter, I am afraid." He flicked his fingers, and she shook her head, because there was much to resolve between them. Grasping her ankles, he dragged her to the edge of the mattress, and she shrieked. "But you must believe me, they were nothing to me, whereas you are everything."

"What are you doing?" When she stood, he turned her around and untied the laces of her gown, which he inched to her waist. "Ernest, I am quite capable of undressing myself, and you cannot sleep here."

"I do not plan to sleep much, and I am sure you are most capable, but I want to do it, as I have often dreamed of this moment." The dress hit the floor, and the chemise, hose, and garters followed. Naked as the day she was born, she blushed, when he led her to stand before the long mirror. "You are so beautiful, Henrietta, and how I have ached to look upon you like this. Indeed, you surpass my wildest fantasies, and trust me there were many, but tonight you became mine, for all time, and I want to celebrate this most cherished occasion." From behind, he cupped her breasts and toyed with her nipples. "Whatever happens in London, you will be my wife. Never doubt that." He smacked her bottom. "Now, climb into bed, because I want you again."

"Ernest, you must be joking, because despite your plans, we should not be doing this." As if she had not noticed his arousal, which he pressed to the cleft of her derriere. "What if we are discovered? What of my reputation? And there are other consequences to consider, given I am an unmarried woman. We cannot engage in such activities again."

"Sweetheart, that is a mere technicality, which will soon be rectified." Despite her warning, he shuffled her to the four-poster and lifted her to the mattress. "And if you think I can blithely return to my chamber, after sampling what you have to offer, you are grossly mistaken. In fact, when we journey to London, I will instruct Crawford to install you in a room close to mine, so that you shall never again pass a night not spent in my arms."

"Is that a promise?" How she needed his strength just then, as their shared passion left her shaken and vulnerable. "Because, if we continue down this perilous path, I need to know this is really happening. I need to know I can depend on you, as I have already risked everything. As you so deftly pointed out, society holds women to a different standard, and without you I am ruined, but you would be free to go about your business. This is not a child's game we play."

"Do you doubt me?" Even as she expressed what she considered grave concerns, which could have catastrophic consequences, he grinned. "That is not very kind of you, my little bird."

"Ernest, I am trying to be serious." Could

he not see that she needed reassurance? As she rested amid the pillows, he reclined at her side and with his hands he roamed her body, and nothing escaped his attention. She should have protested. Should have banished him to his own accommodation, because someone needed to be the voice of reason, but she could not turn him away. The yearning, the hunger swelled, and she cupped his cheek. "We have talked about some wonderful things, and I am counting on you, because I am yours."

"As well you should, given nothing and no one, not even my father, can stop us, now." In that instant, he covered her, nudged apart her legs with his knees, eased his hips to hers, and entered her. "Because this is forever, my only love. My darling Henrietta."

CHAPTER NINE

London

The London Season manifested an array of diversions guaranteed to satisfy the appetites of even the most discriminating member of society. For the men, there were afternoons in the ring, engaging in pugilistic endeavors, at Gentleman Jackson's Saloon, the early evening Promenade in the park, where most rakes hunted their next mistresses, the nightly balls, where the same rogues made their play for their intended targets, brandy taken at White's, where the scoundrels bragged and lied of their prowess, and for the more lascivious cravings, there were the gaming halls and houses of ill repute that catered to every desire, no matter how vulgar. But their chief concern was avoiding the marriage-minded mamas of the *ton*.

For the society ladies, life in the city presented an altogether different experience that revolved around being seen at their best. There were afternoon teas, the same jaunts through the park, evening musicales, nightly balls and visits to Almack's, but the mission was entirely different, which put them at odds with their male counterparts. Their primary goal was to secure a husband, either for themselves or an unattached relation.

It was that spirited competition, neither frivolous nor grave, that led Ernest to choose the Netherton's annual celebration for Henrietta's coming out, and although she would not be presented at court, in the official ceremony, he resolved to observe a singular custom to mark the joyous occasion. After a visit to the hothouse, he returned to Howe House, with a box containing a posy made of three pristine, white blooms.

"Good evening, brother." Barrington lingered in the foyer, a habit that foreboded an impending lecture, of some sort. "May I have a word with you in my study?"

"What have I done now?" Drawing his watch from his pocket, he checked the time, as he strolled down the hall, in Barrington's wake. "Can it not wait, as I need to dress for the ball, and I would not be late?"

"No, it cannot wait." In the man's sanctuary, Barrington folded his arms and leaned against his desk. Ernest was in trouble. "I have been meaning to speak to you about your nightly forays into Henrietta's private chamber." Blushing, he opened and then closed his mouth. "That did not come out as I intended it, but I knew I should have protested, when you insisted she be given a room not three doors from yours."

"No need to explain, as I get your meaning." In silence, Ernest cursed, because he thought he had been discreet. "What gave us away?"

"You must be joking." Barrington snorted. "Her scream of passion in the wee hours startled me and Florence awake, only this morning, and such behavior reflects poorly on you, given you are older and wiser. But the servants will hold Hen responsible, and I will not have it, so you will cease your games until you are married."

"I will not, and the entire matter is none of your affair." Ah, a fresh recollection of his lady's achingly sweet cries filled his ears, as he rode her just before dawn, and he sighed. When Barrington slammed a fist to his blotter, Ernest started and came alert.

"Before you rip at me, you must understand that mine is not an act of rebellion. The simple truth is I am happy, brother. For the first time, in a long time, I am happy, and I have Henrietta to thank for that. And do not ask me to temper my actions, where she is concerned, because I cannot, as I love her."

"Do you think me blind?" Barrington rolled his eyes. "Of course, I know you love her. Bloody hell, you practically ooze honey whenever she is near, and if you continue down that path, you will attract the attention of the entire *ton*, before you are prepared to answer for her. And heaven help you if rumors reach the mews and Graham discovers you have well and thoroughly compromised his daughter. If that happens, it is doubtful even I could save you."

"Then I should talk to him, which is long overdue, because I would still have his blessing." And it would not be easy, but Ernest had to try, for Henrietta's sake. "But I live in the open now. No more worrying about appearances and what everyone thinks. I have spent too much of my life endeavoring to sustain society's good opinion, yet they turned their backs on me in my darkest hour."

"Are you sure about that?" At the side table, Barrington lifted a crystal decanter and poured two glasses of brandy, one of which he offered to Ernest. "Old habits are hard to break, and you have long defined yourself by your reputation. Can you surrender it so easily?"

"To marry the woman of my dreams?" Ernest snickered. "There is no choice, and I will not return to my bed, just to keep up appearances. Indeed, I cannot sleep without Hen in my arms, and I promised her she would never again pass a night outside my embrace."

"Then I would caution you, one last time, to guard your habits where Henrietta is concerned." Barrington averted his stare. "Given I seized Florence's prize before our nuptials, I am the last person to cast stones, but I took drastic measures to ensure no one knew of our regular rendezvous. For the love of all creation, cover her mouth with your hand, when she nears completion. Do whatever you must, but keep her quiet."

"All right." Of course, that was easier said than done, because he thrilled to her boisterous approbations of his skills between the sheets, but they had the rest of their lives to enjoy connubial pleasures. With that, he headed for the exit. "If you will excuse me, I should like to give the posy to Henrietta, that she might fix it to her gown, for the ball."

"One more thing, brother." Barrington gave Ernest pause. "It does my heart good to see you so happy, and I would hate for anything to spoil that."

"Thank you." Ernest gazed at his brother and nodded an acknowledgment. "I never supposed this would come about, and I will not give her up without a fight, because without her I am dead to this world."

Myriad thoughts battled for his attention, on the heels of his morbid declaration, as he returned to the foyer. On the hall tree hung a couple of riding crops, and he became aware that he had delayed a confrontation with Graham out of some misplaced sense of duty, because he desperately needed the stablemaster's approval, though he knew not why. Underlying his trepidation was a deep-seated fear of rejection. The servant had already made his position clear, when it came to a union between Ernest and Henrietta, but he never comprehended the reason for the objection.

"May I be of service, Lord Ernest?" Crawford clasped his hands.

"Deliver this to Miss Graham, and instruct her to wear it, tonight." Ernest gave the box with the posy into the butler's care. "Tell her

I shall await her arrival in the drawing room, at approximately seven-thirty."

"Yes, my lord." Crawford bowed and ascended the grand staircase, leaving Ernest alone to reflect on his situation.

He was crossing the gardens before he realized he had moved, and a single question occupied him to the detriment of all else. It was time to discover the answer behind Graham's repudiation, and Ernest would not leave until he found satisfaction.

A couple of stable hands loitered about the mews, cleaning stalls, brushing horses, tending the tack, and polishing saddles. To the rear sat the small quarters in which the staff resided when the family journeyed to London. At the tiny portal, he knocked on the oak panel, and Graham appeared shortly thereafter.

"My lord, how may I help you?" The stablemaster lowered his chin and stared at the ground.

"Have you a moment to spare for a private conversation?" Ignoring the fast-rising panic he could not deflect, Ernest stepped inside the modest accommodation. "Please, sir."

"Who am I to refuse you, my lord?" A hint of disdain colored Graham's response, to which Ernest would have taken exception under different circumstances. "As always, I am at your service."

"It is about Henrietta and our impending marriage." Like a nervous beggar, Ernest shuffled his feet. "I would ask for your blessing, for her sake, but I would also know the source of your opposition. Why did you conspire to separate us? What have you against me, the second son of a marquess?" When the stablemaster hesitated, Ernest added, "I would have you speak freely, without fear of retribution."

Silence weighed heavy.

"In the sennight preceding Henrietta's departure from Garring Manor, I happened upon a shocking scene I could not begin to explain in a rational sense, and given the differences in our respective statures, I expected my daughter would bear the blame, if discovered." The stablemaster sat at a small table and extended a hand, thus Ernest eased to the other chair. "Out of sheer desperation and a desire to protect Henrietta, I decided to apprise your father that, after hearing a strange noise one night, I ferreted the source and located you in her bed."

Dumbfounded by the revelation, Ernest searched his faded memory and recalled the instance that brought him to seek comfort where he always found it, in Hen's arms, and he shook his head. "Even as children, we were as one entity, though I submit, due to our age at the time, our behavior was innocent."

"Be that as it may, I could not risk having my young daughter dragged into a shameful confrontation with Lord Ravenwood, so I made it clear you had to have encroached on our home." Graham rubbed his chin and frowned. "It might interest you to know that His Lordship's first reaction was to fault my girl, despite the fact that she was but a child of eight, too inexperienced and naïve to fathom the implications of her actions, and I had to defend her with every ounce of my strength, against your sire's ridiculous accusations and violent attacks on her character. So I did what I was forced to do—I sent her away. If you must know, I never objected to you. Rather, I will not stand by idly as my daughter is battered and pummeled for the entertainment of those who consider themselves above her."

"And I wholeheartedly support your position, as you did what any caring and supportive father would do for his child." The irony was not lost on Ernest, given his father's abuse. "But I would have you know what drove me to the sanctuary I found in Henrietta's bed, as a boy. And I would impress upon you what keeps me there, as a man."

"So the insinuations are true, and you have ruined Henrietta." Graham clenched and unclenched his fists. "And you call yourself a gentleman."

"Forgive me, sir, as I never intended to besmirch your good name, but your daughter and I are bound by some invisible but powerful connection, and we resumed our relationship from the moment we were reunited." Ernest inhaled a breath and rolled his shoulders. "But I would have you know that I love her. I love her more than my own life, and she is my wife, already, in my estimation. Regardless of what happens tonight, when she makes her come out into society, whether or not the *ton* accepts her, I will wed her."

"What if you beget a babe?" Graham pushed from his seat and paced. "What will you do, then?"

"It is simple." Ernest shrugged. "Return to Garring and marry her, posthaste."

"You are that determined?" When Ernest dipped his chin, Graham narrowed his stare. "Why?"

"For you to understand, if that is at all possible, my dedication to her, I must divulge an ugly truth, which I have kept secret for years, if only to shield my family legacy from scandal." And that was the most brutish aspect of the torture Ernest's father inflicted upon him. The furtive nature of the crime. "There is a sinister sort of compact to physical battery committed by a father upon his son, and chief among the savagery is the silence, although it is not even taught. Rather, it is instinctive, yet it functions as a means of control, because the injured party, too young to fully comprehend the manipulation, defends the one who inflicts the pain. He knows what is happening to him is wrong, but he covers and conceals the evidence, defending the batterer, because he views it as a means of protecting himself. Perhaps, it is the only protection available to him. But there was a small part of him, his truest and most genuine self, that he tucked away, hidden in a place his father could not touch, and he shared that tattered fragment of himself with one person, if only to remember that he was human. That he was deserving of love."

"And that person was Henrietta." It was a statement, not a question, and Graham swore under his breath. "I am so sorry, my lord. Had I known of the abuse, I would have said nothing. I would have tried to help you." Then the stablemaster flinched. "The black eye, the split lip, and the bruises—Lord Ravenwood said you fell from your horse, the day Henrietta departed Derbyshire."

"He beat me almost to death, that afternoon, and I never knew what I did to deserve the punishment, not that he required motivation." Ernest gazed at Graham and smiled. "I should thank you, because you just solved a longstanding conundrum."

"Which I caused, with my inadvertent and innocent admission." Graham cradled his face in his hands. "I cannot apologize enough, my lord."

"It is not your fault, because you could not have known of the repercussions." The weight of the world slipped free from Ernest's soul, as his suffering was at long last acknowledged, and he relaxed and reclined in the chair. "To be honest, I am surprised you did not find us much sooner, because I always ventured to Henrietta's window, such that I cannot even recall when it started, whereupon I crawled into bed with her after my regular whippings, and she consoled me. That is why I will not surrender her, for you or anyone else."

Once again, Graham fell quiet, and he resumed his place at the table. For a few minutes, he studied Ernest, and then he cleared his throat.

"All right." The stablemaster pinned Ernest with the intensity of his glare. "I will support you."

~

Gowned in pale green *eau de Nil* silk trimmed in seed pearls, in a design of her own creation, which she made expressly to compliment the necklace Ernest purchased, with her hair arranged in a crown of curls, Henrietta stood before the long mirror and pinned the charming coming out posy to the bodice, just over her heart, and she hoped Ernest would note the significance of its position.

Nervous but resigned to launch her introduction into society; she gave herself a final inspection and marched to the door. In the hall, she daubed her temples and straightened her spine. With chin held high, she navigated the long corridor, until she came to the landing, whereupon she descended the grand staircase. Halfway down, she halted, because her father lingered in the foyer, along with Ernest.

"Henrietta, you look beautiful." Papa gazed at her with tear-filled eyes. "How I wish your mother was here to see you in your finery, because she would be so proud, as am I."

"Thank you, Father." Unsure what to make of his demeanor, she advanced with caution. To Ernest, so handsome in his black formalwear, she said, "My lord, fie on you, as you outshine me."

"That is not possible." He winked. "And I am beginning to think I need to carry a sword, to fight off all the swains who will surely vie for your attention, because I am of a very jealous nature when it comes to you."

"Posh. Who will notice me, with you at my side?" As a dutiful fiancée, she adjusted his cravat and smoothed the lapels of his coat. "Perhaps I should have sewn a pocket to conceal a pistol, because I shall brook no debutantes infringing on my man."

"I adore you." Ernest kissed her forehead. "Before we depart, I would have you speak with your father, as he has something to say that pertains to us, both."

"But I am still angry with him." From her perspective, her father betrayed her, in the worst possible way, and she knew not how to trust him again. "Would you have us commence our special night with an argument?"

"Please, darling." To her chagrin, Ernest deployed his lethal pout. "Do it for me."

"Very well." On guard for more disapproval, when she already felt so vulnerable, she addressed her father with great reluctance. "What have you to say, Papa?"

"Only that I am so sorry for the pain I caused you and Lord Ernest, because I informed the late Lord Ravenwood that I found his youngest son in your bed, and that is why he insisted I remove you from the property, else he would do it for me." Her father shuffled his feet and bowed his head. "I feared for your safety, given the growing attachment between you, so I tried to forestall any trouble. Had I known the reason Lord Ernest sought your company, I would have acted differently, and I regret what happened."

"Oh, Papa, how could you have exposed us like that, when Ernest suffered at Lord Ravenwood's hands for years?" In that moment, her heart sank, and she leaned against Ernest for support. "We were just children."

"I know I made a grave mistake, and I can never make amends, but there is something I can do, if you let me." Her father's contrition wrenched her gut. "I would give my blessing to your union, because I was wrong, and I am man enough to admit it."

"You would do that for us?" Without hesitation, she reached for her father, and he splayed his arms. As she always had, she rushed into his familiar and comforting embrace. "You champion us, because I do so need you?"

"My child, I may be old and set in my ways, but I love you." Papa pressed his lips to her hair and patted her back. "We can talk tomorrow. Now, go and make your debut, and remember you are a Graham. We are made of sterner stuff, and if society does not like you, they can go to the devil."

"*Papa.*" Heaving a sigh of relief, because she hated being at odds with her father, she kissed his coarse cheek. "Thank you. Your support means more than you will ever know."

"I, for one, agree with your father." Ernest draped her pelisse about her shoulders and offered his escort, which she accepted. "But I predict you will take London by storm, and we will be the most marvelous couple by the end of the Season."

"I wish I shared your confidence." As she

crossed the threshold, she glanced at her father, and he blew her a kiss.

As a young girl, she traveled to London with her father, and she shared a room with a maid, downstairs. Often, she huddled in the shadows, admiring the former Lady Ravenwood dressed in her best gowns, bedecked in shimmering jewels, and coiffed to perfection, as she departed for the balls. Never would Henrietta have imagined walking the same path to the awaiting coach, which boasted the Ravenwood coat of arms.

Sinking in the squabs, she settled her skirts, as Ernest eased to the space beside her. Then Florence and Barrington occupied the opposite bench, the footman closed the door and secured the latch, and the graceful equipage lurched forward, carrying the stablemaster's daughter to her first social event.

"How did everything go?" Barrington inquired, in a soft voice.

"Very well." Ernest gave her a gentle nudge. "Graham gave us his blessing, and my fetching fiancée has reconciled with her father, so all is stupendous as we embark on our adventure."

"Oh, Henrietta, I am so excited for you." Florence bounced in her seat and narrowed her stare. "That ensemble is stunning. You simply must make me some gowns, as your work is superb, and I daresay every debutante in London will kill to know your designer."

"I told her we should purchase a storefront on Bond Street and hire a small army of seamstresses to create her unique fashions." Ernest took her hand in his and squeezed her fingers. "With her artistic talents and my financial genius, we could make a fortune."

"Is that all you think about?" In play, she elbowed him. "Does polite society not frown on those in trade?"

"I am not sure it will matter." Florence leaned forward and studied Hen's attire. "Your skills are *sans pareil*, and every matchmaking mama will want you to create something spectacular to help their daughter stand above the rest in the marriage mart."

"Florence is right. With the mamas, when it comes to their little angels, money is no object." Barrington kicked Ernest. "And you always find a way to make a profit."

"I do." Ernest grinned, just as the coach came to a halt. "Well, my little bird, it is time to make your grand entrance upon the London stage. Are you ready?"

"As ever, I suppose." Holding her breath, she stepped from the rig, and Ernest handed her to the sidewalk. When she noted the palatial residence, she almost tripped. "Ernest, I do not think I can go through with it."

"Just stay by my side, and everything will be fine." He led her into the entry hall, where a receiving line welcomed the revelers. "Believe me, you belong here, Henrietta. Never let anyone convince you otherwise."

In a whirl of activity, she navigated the crush, until they reached the ballroom, whereupon the butler announced their arrival. From a distance, her name came to her, and her ears rang, like the bells in a Wren steeple. And into the throng she walked.

Elegantly garbed ladies and gentlemen milled about the chasmal chamber, which boasted cut glass chandeliers and ornate tapestries in a style unlike any she had ever seen, and she made her beau take a tour of the room, so she could admire the décor.

"Why does no one notice the furnishings?" she whispered. "The carpet pattern would make a gorgeous trim for a gown. Does no one recognize the impeccable splendor, or do they take it all for granted?"

"I imagine it is lost on those who were born to such privilege, my little bird." He strolled to the terrace doors, so she could stroke the velvet drapes. "Perhaps that is what I love most about you."

"I am so glad to hear you say it." In awe of her surroundings, she almost forgot where she was, and she quickly came alert. "Whatever happens, thank you, for bringing me here. It is a night I shall never forget."

As per Ernest's advice, as he introduced her, she shared naught of her history. Instead, she remained coy and quiet, and that seemed to attract even more attention, especially when the music and dancing commenced, and she found herself beset upon by an army of hopeful partners.

"Well, it is official. You are all the rage, my dear." The intensity of Ernest's appraisal conveyed appreciation of a different sort, and she braced for another in a long line of salacious suggestions. If she were lucky, he would not disappoint her, because she did so enjoy his ravishment. "And I cannot wait to get you home and peel you out of that dress, but I would have you leave on the pearls when I make love to you."

"Oh?" Cursing the telltale burn of a blush, she stuck her tongue in her cheek. "Will it enhance your performance, because I am not sure you can improve on perfection?"

"Flattery will get you everywhere, my

tempting vixen." Ah, she treasured his flirtation. "And I must confess I envisioned you naked, wearing naught but the necklace, when I purchased it."

"Scandalous, my lord." How she ached to kiss him just then. "And I shall endeavor to fulfill your wish, tonight."

"Brother, Florence bade me to warn you to stop undressing Henrietta with your eyes, because you attract the wrong sort of attention." Barrington wagged a finger. "And no more dances, as you claimed two, already."

"What if they play another waltz?" Ernest scowled, and she giggled. "I cannot abide another man holding my woman."

"Is she your woman?" A vaguely familiar face intruded on the conversation, and then he gazed directly at her. "Hello, Henrietta. It has been a long time."

"*Percy.*" She just stopped herself from leaping at Ernest's cousin. "Is it really you?"

"Indeed, it is, old friend." As would a gentleman, he took her hand in his and pressed a chaste kiss to her gloved knuckles. "I could not believe it, when I got Barrington's note, but I was glad to receive it. And here you are, in the flesh, no less. My, what a picture you present, such that I almost did not recognize you." To Ernest, Percy said, "May I have this dance with your lady?"

"You may." Ernest folded his arms. "But bring her back to me, afterward."

"You have my solemn promise, cousin." Percy crossed his heart and then led her into the rotation. "It is wonderful to see you, again, Hen. We have missed your spirited nature, which is something our family needs, right now."

"And what about you? I was disappointed when I did not find you at Garring, when I arrived." She marveled at his patrician features, his customary Howe blond locks, and his brilliant blue eyes tinged with a hint of sadness. "Ernest told me of your mother. I am so very sorry."

"Yes, it was a horrid disgrace, and I am still shunned by some, thus I often stay home and avoid unwanted attention." Given Percy's amiable personality, she could not understand how anyone could snub him, which she likened to kicking a pup. "But I will persevere, just as you did. By the by, Ernest explained the situation, in detail, and I stand at the ready, to do whatever I can to help you to the altar."

"As usual, you are very kind." In his company, she found an ally, because they were both outcasts, of a sort. "And I pledge to do the same for you, dear friend."

"Do you believe someone could love me, the way you love Ernest?" Of course, he would know of her devotion, because they were playmates, as children. "Because I would have a family of my own, someday."

"If it can happen for me, it can happen for anyone." When the music ended, she sought Ernest, and he waved, as if she could miss him. "Is there any particular lady who has caught your notice?"

"There is, and perhaps you can catch her for me, as I suspect she is similarly tortured." He chuckled. "But for now I see your impatient swain, as he paces, thus I had better return you to him, before he runs amok."

Back on Ernest's arm, Henrietta savored the tasty delights at dinner, making conversation as though she belonged in such estimable company. Later, she hid behind an ornamental screen, as her man fed her delicious bites of a sumptuous lemon tart, interspersed with even more delectable kisses.

All too soon, the long case clock chimed the midnight hour, and once again she found herself safely ensconced in the Ravenwood coach, bound for Howe House and the bed she shared with Ernest. Leaning against him, she yawned.

"My darling, you were a smashing success." He twined his fingers in hers. "I believe we may have worried for nothing, and your first London Season will be a triumph."

CHAPTER TEN

In the fortnight since Henrietta made her stellar debut, the London gossip mill featured countless speculations regarding her background, and Ernest ruthlessly guarded her history. At the same time, he reveled in her success, because her gentle spirit, innate poise, and unique fashions made her the darling of the Season. With everything going according to plan, and nary a mishap, he prepared a few final outings guaranteed to secure her place in society.

"Florence will be down in a half hour, which gives us time to settle our business." Barrington joined Ernest, as he sat in one of the high back chairs situated before the hearth, in the study. "I advised my solicitor to make the last transfer of funds to repay the debt on Garring Manor."

"I have told you that is not necessary." And it irked Ernest that his brother refused to accept the money as a gift. "I am part of this family, if you recall."

I know that." Barrington opened a drawer, drew forth a document, affixed his signature, rolled the parchment, and brought the item to Ernest. "But the marquessate is my responsibility, and this fulfills my duty. Do not mistake my meaning, because this is not an issue of finance. It is a matter of principle."

"If you insist." Despite inclinations to the contrary, he took the receipt and folded it flat, before pocketing it. And while he loathed discussing such dealings, nothing could dampen his excitement. "So we are ready for another in a series of triumphant social engagements?"

"That reminds me, I have been meaning to talk to you about Henrietta." Not again. Barrington eased to the other seat, rested his elbow on the armrest, and cradled his chin in his palm. "I know you have the best of intentions, but I do not like how you have restyled her. She is not herself, and I do not think she is happy. For what it is worth, Florence agrees with me, and we are left to wonder if you want Hen, our old friend and the stablemaster's daughter, or what you believe you can make of her?"

"I beg your pardon?" While Barrington's assertions rankled, he had a point, but it was for her own good that Ernest recreated her in a more polished version. "Can you not see that it is for the best? If I am to give her the life she deserves, and I would give her everything, we must promote the ruse, else society will shun her."

"What if you lose her, in the process?" Of course, Barrington had to pose the one question that kept Ernest awake at night. Although he remained steadfast in his opinion on the subject, he noticed a tad less joy in his lady's expression, of late, and he resolved to make it up to her, once they were safely wed and installed in their new summer home, far from the prying eyes of the *ton*. And when she enjoyed the protection of his good name, no one would dare attack her. Barrington slapped his thigh, and Ernest started. "Are you listening to me?"

"Yes, and I understand your concern, but it will all be over with, soon." Until then, Ernest would hold his breath. "Besides, Henrietta wants what I want, and if she felt otherwise, she would have told me, but she raised no objections. Indeed, she supports and stages our charade. Is that not proof enough of her sentiment?"

"I wonder if she does so because it is what you want?" Shifting his weight, Barrington stretched his booted feet. "She would do anything for you, even if it meant destroying herself, and that is what worries me. And what of your new perspective? I thought you no longer cared for appearances? Did you not sit in my study at Garring and assert your independence? Does that freedom not extend to Hen?"

"I did, and it does." In that instant, he pushed from the chair and paced before the hearth. Raking his fingers through his hair, he groaned. "If only you knew what I surrendered of my character to protect this family in your most grievous hour, you would not be so quick to judge me."

"To what do you refer?" Barrington inclined his head and sobered when Ernest remained mute. "What have you done?"

"It is nothing." Ernest did not want to have that conversation, and he apprehended, too late, that he spoke in frustration and haste. "You need not worry about what you cannot change."

"Ernest, I spent five years as a pirate, on the run from a vicious crime I did not commit, worrying about things I could not change, only to learn that nothing is certain, and everything is negotiable when it comes to fate." Barrington stood and blocked Ernest's stride. "You would be surprised by what can be undone, if you try hard enough, and redemption can be found where you least expect it."

"It does not signify." When Ernest tried to make his escape, Barrington refused to yield. "You do not understand. I promised myself I would never reveal my nefarious deed, because I would not have you believe I thought the worst of you, when my actions were driven by convictions to the contrary."

"This has something to do with the murder." Pain flitted through Barrington's usually carefree countenance, and he furrowed his brow. "Tell me what you did. What confidence do you conceal, and have you not tucked away enough secrets for two lifetimes? Given what you hid for our father, what you shielded from scrutiny that he might continue his unchecked assaults on your person without fear of retribution, how can you keep anything from me?"

"You think me so proper, so invested in my reputation that I walk the straight and narrow path, and that is what motivates my plans, in regard to Henrietta, but you could not be more wrong." It was as if heaven and earth conspired against Ernest, to waylay his strategy and undermine his fortitude, when the truth was he was not half so sure of himself or his scheme, because there were still so many things that could go awry. "You want to know how far I went to protect you? To what lengths I conspired to ensure you were not arrested for the homicide, when I knew, beyond a shadow of a doubt, you were innocent?" He turned, rested his hands against the mantelshelf, gazed into the blaze, and opened the door to his memory. What he found still possessed unerring power to hurt him. "It was early that morning, when I was roused from sleep by a scream of terror, and nothing has been the same since that dreadful day. When Ashby informed me of the body found in your bed, I panicked, especially because you were not home."

"I was with Florence." Barrington cast a wistful smile. "But you did not know that, then."

"Can you not see my dilemma? My only motive was protecting you, my brother, the person whose life is more dear to me than my own, so I did what I could to defend you." Swallowing hard, Ernest clenched and unclenched his fists. "I stole the murder weapon, which I found on the floor, near the foot of your bed. In a handkerchief I enfolded the bloody knife, which I later threw into the Thames." Closing his eyes, he revisited that night, as a howling gale from an encroaching storm played a morbid accompaniment. "Now you see I am not so proper as you believe. Indeed, I am a desperate man, so close to achieving my long-cherished goal that there is nothing I would not do, there is no price I am not willing to pay to win the woman of my dreams and build a life I once thought possible only in the realm of fantasy. Have I not earned it? Have I not paid in the coin of bloody flesh, a thousand times over?"

"You fought too many battles in your youthful existence, and my biggest regret is that I wasted my formative years mired in self-absorption and insouciant endeavors unbecoming a gentleman of rank, when I should have defended you." When Barrington draped an arm about Ernest's shoulders and gave a gentle nudge, he flinched. "As the older brother, our positions should have been reversed. I should have taken care of you, but you were always the one who looked after me. I can only hope it is not too late to make amends."

"What do you propose?" In that moment, Ernest perceived himself much as he had when he wore shortcoats. "And I am a bit too old for a nanny."

"Ah, but you are never too old to wrestle your brother." Barrington snickered, and it was the only warning Ernest got.

In seconds, he found himself bent forward, as Barrington ruffled Ernest's hair, and he lunged to the side. Barrington chuckled, as they toppled a table, and Ernest seized the advantage. After delivering a quick jab to Barrington's ribs, Ernest leaned to the side, yanked his brother off balance, and they ended up rolling on the floor, laughing the entire time.

"What on earth is going on in here?" Lying on his back, Ernest gazed at Florence, who loomed in the doorway, with Henrietta to the right. "Have a couple of feral hounds invaded Howe House? Upon my word, but are you two not beyond such childish behavior?"

"Indeed." Henrietta clutched her throat but appeared to be staving off mirth. "Ernest Cornelius Frederick, get up and dust off your coat, as we are ready to depart for Gunter's, and you promised I could sample a variety of delicious ices."

"Oh, I love it when you use that *governessy* tone with me, my little bird." He could not help but taunt her, when she cut the perfect picture of an elegant society lady, in a pale blue gown of her own design, with her signature hand-painted flowers at the sleeves and hem. As he stood, he made no attempt to veil his appraisal, and she rewarded him with her characteristic blush. "And I was just teaching Barrington a lesson in personal defense."

"Ha!" Barrington chucked Ernest's chin. "More like I schooled you, scamp."

"Who are you calling a scamp, Iron Corsair?" Yes, Ernest went for the gut, but he could not resist the temptation. "Do you not have some booty to plunder?"

"A lot you know." Barrington caught Florence about the waist, pulled her close, and kissed her with a loud smack. "I plunder and maraud some priceless booty, every morning and night."

"*Barrington.*" Florence slapped his hand, even as she giggled. "Behave, and let us go, as I am craving the *neige de pistachio,* and I intend to indulge in a double portion, because I am eating for two."

"All right, my darling wife." Barrington led her into the hall. "You may have whatever you desire, because your every wish is my command."

Alone with Henrietta, Ernest stood tall, as she adjusted his cravat, a habit she displayed with greater frequency and harkened to a devoted bride. Given his conversation with Barrington, Ernest wanted to ask her a few pointed questions. Just as he opened his mouth, his brother beckoned. So instead, he simply said, "Shall we depart?"

~

Occupying a prime position in Berkley Square, Gunter's Tea Shop had cultivated a well-earned reputation as purveyors of some of the finest English, French, and Italian sweetmeats, and Henrietta had long wanted to sample their wares, but such luxuries were beyond the means of a simple stablemaster's daughter. However, as the future wife of an estimable member of the *ton*, an afternoon visit to the famous Mayfair vendor functioned as another in an extended list of requisite social gatherings, and she was not about to complain. Sitting at a table near the window, in a prime location, Henrietta bit her lip, when the server delivered the selections, which looked too pretty to eat.

Fascinated by the exquisite porcelain, she ran her finger along the gold-trimmed edge.

"Is this Sèvres china?"

"Yes." Florence snatched an odd-shaped ice and did not bother with a spoon. Rather, she bit the top off the bulbous confection, closed her eyes, and hummed her appreciation. "Oh, this is pure heaven."

"And what are the dishes called, because I have never seen anything like them?" The cups with miniature platforms presented the desserts as tiny statues, of a sort.

"They are *tasses à glace*, situated on a *plateau au bouret*." Florence manifested a treasure trove of information, and she always answered Henrietta's litany of queries with a wealth of patience and understanding, as she repeated her answer, taking care to emphasize the correct pronunciation. "But you will not be expected to plate ices with such precision, when you host guests at home."

"How am I ever going to remember everything required of my new station?" Surrounded by the gilt and glitter of London, she hoped she might one day view herself as one of the beautiful people, but in that moment she remained lost.

"Are you all right?" Ernest furrowed his brow, as he dug his spoon into the bergamot ice. "As you appear out of sorts, my little bird."

"I am fine." And if she told herself that enough, she just might believe it. Then she noted the lines of strain about his usually animated eyes. "Why do you ask? Is something wrong?"

"No." He smiled, but for some reason she suspected he felt otherwise. For a minute, he just looked at her. Then he leaned near. "Are you happy?"

"Of course." At least, she thought she was happy. She wanted to be happy. Regardless of the nagging doubts, of one thing she was certain. She wanted to make Ernest happy. "What a strange question."

"Are you sure?" Beneath the shield of the tablecloth, he covered her hand with his. "Because I do so want you to be happy, Hen. But if you are not, you can tell me, and we can figure out another way. I promise, I will not be angry. Please, talk to me."

"My lord, it is not necessary to alter your strategy, because your plan succeeds, even now." Perhaps that was why she did not trust the situation. It seemed too easy. Still, that was not his fault. And was that not what she wanted? "While I will admit to some discomfit, because, at the end of the day, I am the stablemaster's daughter, and I do not imagine I will ever quite fit in society, I will do whatever it takes to be a wife of which you are proud to call your own."

"I am already proud, sweetheart." When he studied her lips, she shifted in her seat, because she could read him like a book. "And I would wed you in naught but your chemise, as you know I prefer you in that—and much less."

"*Ernest*." Without thought for propriety, she mirrored Florence's actions and snatched the *épine-vinette*. With her tongue, she trailed the plumb-shaped tip of the protuberant ice, and he groaned and flexed his fingers. It was then she noted the no doubt unintended conformity to a particular part of his anatomy. Fresh images burst to life, as she recalled a particularly salacious tutorial, after the Richmond's gala. "I know what you reference, and I am not ashamed of it, because nothing we share strikes me as forbidden. Is it always like that?"

"I think, for us, it is to be expected, because of our longstanding devotion." He handed her a spoon. "But I cannot resist the temptation you pose, and I am liable to spread you, here and now, atop the table, lift your ankles and have my wicked way with you, so you should observe the proprieties, just this once."

"That would certainly give the gossipmongers something to talk about." The stress investing her frame vanished, and she relaxed and savored the delicious treat. "So what is next on our agenda?"

"The Hogart musicale, in a fortnight." Rolling his eyes, he snorted. "While you may never forgive me for exposing you to such a vicious mutilation of your delicate ears, because the twins possess an artistic talent that defies efforts to describe it, and I assert there are no words to do it justice, I would argue such an event is a right of passage for any prospective member of the *ton*, and I promise I will make it up to you, that night, when we return to Howe House. What say I teach you a new tack? I may employ a new Latin term."

"Given you have proven yourself quite capable, in that respect, and I am always anxious to know more, I will hold you to it." She giggled and then whispered, "But I would ask that we confine our activities to my bed, because the scrapes to my bottom have yet to heal from our last foray on the rug." Just as Henrietta reached for her cup of tea, two impressive ladies, bearing more than a passing resemblance, approached the group, and Barrington and Ernest stood and bowed.

"Good afternoon, Lord and Lady Ravenwood. Permit me to congratulate you on the impending arrival of your second child." The meticulously coiffed woman, arm in arm with the other, inclined her head, which intensified a regal bearing Hen envied. "And may I inquire after your new friend?"

"Your Graces, we are honored, and we are past due for a visit, which I shall rectify with an open invitation to call upon Howe House, at your leisure." Florence dipped her chin. "Allow me to introduce Miss Henrietta Katherine Graham, a friend of our family and soon to be more than that, if we are lucky." She glanced at Hen and said, "This is Her Grace, the Duchess of Rylan, and Her Grace, the Duchess of Weston."

Unsure how to respond, whether or not she should stand and curtsey, Henrietta remained stock-still and eyed her beau, for guidance. When he ever so slightly nodded, she followed suit.

"She is charming, Lord Ernest." To Henrietta, the duchess of Rylan said, "And I am pleased to make your acquaintance. If it is not too forward, I should like to know the designer of your unique gown, as my sister and I agree it is stunning. Indeed, we could not stop admiring it, from across the room, given the craftsmanship is first rate, and I hope we did not offend you."

"You wish to know about my dress?" Panic traipsed her spine, gripping her in an invisible but nonetheless potent veil of fear, because she knew not how to reply. "Well—"

"I believe she purchased the item in Kent, at a boutique that has since closed its doors, after the proprietor passed away." Barrington glanced at Henrietta and winked. "And where are Rylan and Weston? I still owe them a brandy, after the service they provided to my wife and I, during our difficult courtship. The debt remains, and I should settle my account."

"Posh, Lord Ravenwood." The duchess of Weston caught Henrietta's attention, because the noblewoman was missing an arm, as evidenced by the empty sleeve pinned to her bodice. "We were glad to be of service, and His Grace benefits from a bit of mischief, every now and then, as he is quite the stodgy character, but I am working on him."

"And that reminds me, we are late." The duchess of Rylan turned and almost bumped into Agnes Dudley. "I beg your pardon, madam."

"Oh, Your Grace, it was entirely my fault, as I wanted to compliment you on your sense of style and refined taste. Agnes Dudley, of

the Derbyshire Dudleys, at your service."
Mrs. Dudley stared down her nose at the
duchess of Weston. "And it is wonderful to
see you, too, Your Grace. I could not help
but overhear your conversation, and I share
your appreciation of Miss Graham's attire."

Henrietta almost fell from her chair.

"Thank you." The duchess of Weston
compressed her lips. "If you will excuse us,
we were just leaving."

"As were we, and I am tired." Florence
stood, made a none-too-subtle point to ignore
the Dudleys, and Barrington drew her to his
side. "My lord, will you summon our
carriage?"

"At once." Barrington shuffled through
the crowd.

Ernest snapped his fingers and a server
responded. After a brief, quiet conversation,
he settled the bill and motioned for Henrietta
to join Florence, and together they exited the
tearoom.

Wringing her fingers, Henrietta feared she
might be ill, and her mind raced, as she
wondered what breach in decorum she
committed. By the time the rig arrived, her
knees buckled, and she shuddered,
uncontrollably. When Ernest handed her into
the squabs, she tripped and almost fell, face

first, onto the pavement, but his quick thinking and unshakable support saved her from further embarrassment.

Ensconced in the privacy of the Ravenwood coach, Florence huffed. "Grasping, vulgar woman."

"I am sorry." Tears welled and spilled down Henrietta's cheeks, given she could not discern her mistake. "While I know not what I did, I apologize and beg your forbearance."

"You think me angry with you?" Florence pressed a fist to her chest. "Oh, no. Dear Henrietta, you were superb."

"Darling, you did nothing wrong. In fact, I thought you performed brilliantly, given the unanticipated questions regarding your clothes." Ernest cupped Henrietta's chin and brought her gaze to his. "Sweetheart." With his handkerchief, he dried her face. "Florence remarks on Mrs. Dudley's gross break in etiquette, which required her to wait until the Duchess of Rylan first addressed her lesser."

"Indeed." Florence leaned on Barrington's shoulder, and he kissed her forehead. "I almost fainted, when Lenore inquired after your gown, but my handsome husband saved the day, and I shall express my gratitude, this evening, as we have no engagements tonight."

"And I will let you." Barrington shifted

and draped his arm about her. "Because I love you."

As the charming scene played on one side of the coach, Henrietta remained locked in a hellish prison, and she could not stop shaking. "I sincerely believed I embarrassed you."

In a singular fragment in time, everything she worked toward, everything she planned with Ernest could have come crashing down, despite their best intentions and diligence, because so much of society and its myriad norms remained a mystery. And the worst part was she would not have known of impending disaster until it was too late.

When they arrived at Howe House, Barrington exited the carriage and handed Florence down. Ernest stepped to the sidewalk, turned, and lifted Henrietta into his arms. Shuffling her in his grasp, he carried her into the foyer, and she buried her face into the curve of his neck as she wept.

"Crawford, have a hot bath prepared for Miss Graham, and send for her lady's maid." Before the butler could respond, Ernest continued upstairs. At the landing, he veered down the hall that led to her chamber, and he did not halt until he eased her to the bed. "Have Maisy undress you, dismiss her for the night, and then get into the tub. I will return and tend you, myself."

Henrietta wanted to answer him, but she could not stop crying long enough to form a response, so she merely nodded.

"My little bird, please, calm yourself, because I comprehend what lies at the heart of your distress, and I believe I have a solution that will suit us." In an achingly tender expression, which encouraged a fresh spate of tears, because she would go to her grave before disappointing him, he bestowed upon her a gentle kiss. "Now, do as I say, and do not fret, because we will not be long apart, and I will work until dawn to ease your distress."

"I beg your pardon, my lord." Maisy loomed in the entry and averted her stare. "But Crawford bade me report to Miss Graham."

"That is all right, Maisy." With a sly smile Henrietta did not quite understand, Ernest stretched tall but never broke their connection. "You may be the first to wish us merry, because Miss Graham has just consented to be my wife."

CHAPTER ELEVEN

A fortnight had passed, and so much had changed, much to Ernest's delight, and he was so close to victory he could taste it. In the aftermath of the unpleasant scene at Gunter's, and Henrietta's misguided distress born of genuine fear, he came to the conclusion that she was not so keen on his plan as she originally conveyed, despite claims to the contrary, so he altered his tack. After a heated discussion, arguing various solutions, his brother sent a missive to *The Times*, announcing the marriage of Henrietta Katherine Graham, of Tunbridge Wells, Kent, to Lord Ernest Cornelius Frederick Howe, with the wedding to take place on June sixth at St. George's, Hanover Square, at the height of the Season.

Given the banns had been posted, Ernest

followed proper decorum and observed all strictures—outside her bedchamber. But within the walls of her sanctuary, between the soft sheets where they came together and joined their bodies, again and again, they found beautiful, mutual acceptance, unshakeable, as if forged in iron. The attachment, the devotion, and the love he thought he harbored for her grew by seemingly endless bounds, beyond the limits of emotion of which he thought himself capable, and he would let nothing stand in their way.

So all they had to do was dance across the *ton's* ballrooms, smile, and do the pretty for society, for a few more weeks, and they were free. They had already decided to immediately retire to Whitstone, which remained under renovation since he completed the purchase, to avoid further mishaps and spare his provincial lady untoward chagrin, until Florence could school Henrietta in the tangled web known as etiquette, and his bride regained her confidence. Then she would take her rightful place, where she always belonged. Although she was not to the manor born, she was born to be his, just as he belonged to her. That was why they ventured to the Hogart's musicale that evening.

The unparalleled experience, and that was a vast deal more than generous description, offered Henrietta an opportunity to mix and mingle in a relatively safe environment. Given the talent, and that was another far too kind depiction of the Hogart's abilities, which were without equal to say the least, he doubted anyone would be paying attention to his future wife. Thus she could gain a measure of practice with not much required on her part.

It was with that thought in mind that he waited in the foyer for his fiancée. Just as he checked his timepiece, she appeared on the landing, and a shudder of awareness rocked his frame, because he had never beheld such a vision.

"Good evening, my lord." Gowned in a cream masterpiece trimmed in old gold, with clusters of multi-colored flowers painted about the bodice, the only thing she lacked was a pair of wings to complete her angelic profile. "Am I late?"

"You are right on time." In that moment, he envisioned her as she looked that afternoon, when he made love to her, with her brown hair splayed across her pillow, and her sweet breasts jostling in time with his thrusts, and it was all he could do not to throw her over his shoulder and haul her back to her suite. Instead, he met her at the final step, which brought them nose to nose, and he kissed her in a lengthy sashay that barely satisfied his appetite. "Ah, my darling, you are so beautiful I could cry."

"Ernest, I do love you." As she brushed aside the hair from his forehead, she smiled, and his heart skipped a beat. "We are going to make it, are we not?"

"I love you, too, my little bird." He rested his palms to her hips and nipped at her nose. "And, yes, we shall triumph, just as I predict our wedding will be the fête to end all fêtes this Season."

"I am so glad to hear you say that." Shimmering, she skipped down the final step, wound her arm in his, and they departed Howe House, with Barrington and Florence.

After a brief carriage ride, they strolled into the Mayfair townhouse, where Beryl Hogart, a portly woman with salt and pepper hair, waited to greet them.

"Lord Ernest and Miss Graham, welcome to my humble abode. Permit me to congratulate you on your impending nuptials, which is the talk of the town." Wearing a bright purple turban and a matching dress, Mrs. Hogart, known for her charitable soul inasmuch as her less than graceful daughters, gushed. "Imagine my delight when I learned the most notable couple in London deigned to attend our musicale, and you are in for a real treat, because my girls have something very special planned for your entertainment."

"Nonsense, Mrs. Hogart." Oh, Ernest knew it would be entertaining, and he swallowed a snort of laughter. "But Miss Graham and I were honored to receive your invitation, given I have told her so much about the Misses Hogart and their inimitable prowess on the violin and the pianoforte, not to mention Miranda's singular vocals, thus nothing could keep my fiancée from it. And who am I to refuse my bride-to-be?"

In that instant, Henrietta tensed at his side, and she flexed her fingers, belying her composure.

"Miss Graham, you are too kind." Mrs. Hogart retreated and scrutinized Henrietta from top to toe. "And you are wearing one of your unusual fashions, which I have heard much about, but the rumors do not do you justice. I beg you, you must tell me the name of your designer, because my Miranda expects to make her own happy announcement with Sir Archibald Kleinfeld, at the end of the Season. You know he has two-thousand a year."

"How wonderful, Mrs. Hogart." Henrietta dipped her chin. "Felicitations, to you and your family. And I am so pleased to at last make the acquaintance of one of the *ton's grand dames*, such that I am a tad intimidated, and I pray you forgive me."

"Upon my word." Mrs. Hogart pressed a hand to her chest. "But you are a woman of discriminating taste and uncommon judgment, for your age, and I knew the moment I saw you that we would get on famously."

"Now, if you will excuse us, we should secure seats for the performance." Ernest bowed and drew Henrietta into the hall, so Barrington and Florence could enter the line of fire. As they cleared the foyer, he bent his head and whispered, "That was inspiring."

"I am fortunate she presented no great mystery, but she strikes me as harmless." Henrietta nodded to a few notables. "What I do not fathom is how many people showed up for what you described as a violent abuse of the ears and a murderous affront to composers, everywhere."

"That is because the Hogart's reputation precedes them, and this really is the best show in town, although not as they intend." Ernest ushered her to two seats at the end of the back row. "Shall I fetch you a cup of lemonade, before the torture commences?"

"Oh, do not leave me." Panic invested her gaze, and she grabbed his wrist. "I am fine."

"Sweetheart, you must not be afraid." When she yanked him again, he relented and sat. "Really, Hen, you cannot live in fear of what might happen, and this is the most innocuous of engagements. Please, relax and enjoy the night, because I so looked forward to spending time with you."

"You spend plenty of time with me, in my bedchamber, my lord." She giggled, and he knew exactly to what she referred. "In fact, Florence says you and I live in each other's pockets. Is it bad that I prefer it that way?"

"I think, for us, it is very good, and I plan to bury my face between your sumptuous breasts, later." He waggled his brows, when she gasped, and waved, as Barrington and Florence entered the room. "And Flo is one to talk, given she occupies the marquess's suite, and I doubt she has ever slept in her own apartment."

"It is rather warm in here." Florence fanned herself, as she took the seat beside Henrietta. "And I hope this does not go on too late."

"Is there anything I can do to make you more comfortable?" Barrington inquired, as he plopped next to her. "Because your wish is my command."

"You could take me home." Florence drew a handkerchief from her reticule and daubed her temples. "Of course, I am joking, because we are here to support Hen, but we do so under very hard terms, and I will not be held responsible if I revisit my dinner, once the trauma begins."

"Is it truly that foul?" Hen asked, in a soft voice, just as the twins assumed their positions.

"You are about to find out for yourself." Indeed, Ernest hoped what could best be described as a comedy of errors would provide a bit of levity during an otherwise stressful time for his lady. "Brace yourself, darling."

The crowd settled, and a hush fell upon the gathering, as the sisters took up their instruments of destruction. Tension weighed heavy in the air, and then the agony commenced.

On the violin, Miranda Hogart scratched something akin to the shrill noises emitted by two cats rather fond of each other, while Margaret pummeled the ivories as if she were killing flies. Barrington compressed his lips, even as his shoulders trembled, Florence bowed her head and failed to stifle a telltale gurgle of mirth, and Henrietta, wide-eyed and mouth agape, flinched and stared at Ernest, and it was all he could do not to laugh aloud at her reaction.

As the second movement played, Barrington winced, Florence gazed at the floor and wiped a stray tear, and Henrietta grimaced, as she dug her fingers into his arm. At last, mercifully, the first of two scheduled intermissions provided a moment of relief.

"My lord, I owe you an apology." Henrietta shifted her weight, and he admired her bosom, which always distracted him. "I thought you exaggerated, but I see now you underestimated the Hogarts'...skills, and I use the term lightly. Had I known—"

"Good evening, Lord and Lady Ravenwood." A painfully familiar voice intruded on the otherwise charming exchange, and Ernest cursed under his breath, as he stood to greet the pest. "Hello, Lord Ernest and Miss Graham. I was surprised to read the news of your wedding, and I would offer my sincere congratulations, along with a member of my family." Agnes Dudley lifted her chin, in an unmistakable air of superiority that grated his last nerve, and turned to another woman. "Permit me to introduce my sister, Bertha Bland of Tunbridge Wells."

Before he could acknowledge the unwelcomed interlopers, Bertha stuck out her finger and pointed at Henrietta. "I know that fashion." Then Ms. Bland wrinkled her nose and squinted through her spectacles. "You are no lady of quality. Why, you are a seamstress from Kent, and I remember your aunt." She sneered and then glanced about the room, as if preparing to impart a dirty little secret. "Miss Graham is in trade."

"Madam, control yourself." Ernest charged the fore, as Henrietta slowly rose from her chair.

The crowd quieted, and a chorus of whispers pervaded the assembly.

One by one, all gazes focused on the unfortunate altercation, which threatened to bring down his fiancée, and he sought the nearest escape but found none. Indeed, all he could do was watch the ensuing confrontation.

"She is an imposter." Bertha shrieked, as if Henrietta were some sort of criminal. "And I wager she made that dress she wears, because she cannot possibly afford the work of a better designer."

"How dare you, as I am no imposter." Henrietta squared her shoulders, ignoring his pleas for forbearance, and he suspected he knew what would happen next, based on her demeanor. When he clutched her by the wrist, she wrenched free. "Yes, I made my gown, and I am quite proud of it. And, yes, I made an honest living, working for my dearly departed aunt, in her boutique. But if you think that beneath you, then you will be further troubled by the fact that I am also a stablemaster's daughter, and I would match my character against yours, any day of the week and twice on Sunday."

~

It was late when Henrietta stirred in the quiet solitude of her bedchamber. Rolling to the side, she discovered she remained fully clothed, and she swung her legs over the edge of the mattress and stood.

After the scene that spoiled the Hogart's musicale, Ernest and Henrietta, along with Barrington and Florence, made a less than elegant exit, to a noticeable symphony of murmurs, from the event. As so many violent emotions thrashed and swirled within her, the rest of the family remained stoic, and for her the silence functioned as a death knell to her short-lived courtship and introduction to

London society, although no one said as much.

In the long mirror, she studied her reflection and the delicate garment she created.

No matter what Agnes Dudley and Bertha Bland said, Henrietta took enormous pride in the unique items she fashioned, and no one could shame her for that. But her actions, however unfairly motivated, reflected negatively on Ernest, and she vowed never to embarrass him. Given she revealed the truth of her birth, and his desire to live in society, she doubted he would marry her, especially as he had not come to her, and that spoke volumes.

Because she had never spent a night bereft of his warm and reassuring embrace, since they reunited, after he made his pledge to that effect. So she resolved to make the separation as easy as possible, because she endured enough drama for two lifetimes.

From the armoire, she drew a carriage dress made of grey wool, as well as several other personal belongings. At the vanity, she removed the diamond ear fobs and the delicate bracelet Ernest gifted her. With a few twists and turns, she loosened her laces and stripped off the dress.

Frowning at the heavy trunk that conveyed her things to Howe House, she opted to borrow a couple of pillowcases, which she snatched from the four-poster. Since Ernest purchased the material for her clothes, she selected only those articles she could not live without, leaving behind the most expensive apparel, in the event he could resell them and reclaim some of his money.

Once she changed into the traveling dress, she fetched her lesser quality boots, which she tied tight, and then lined up the fancy slippers. With a final check of the room, she smoothed the plush counterpane and paused at the footboard, to revisit precious memories.

"Oh, Ernest." Tears beckoned, but she swallowed hard and stood upright, determined to make things right. "You will never know how much I love you."

In that moment, something inside her fractured, sending minute cuts, lethal in their assault, spreading through her, but she would not be deterred. Because she could not survive a confrontation with and a rejection from her beau. So she would run away. She would flee to some place where no one knew her name, and she could be whatever she wanted to be, including a stablemaster's daughter, without fear of recrimination or censure, thus she turned on a heel, grabbed the stuffed bundles, and sprinted from the room.

A single taper lit the hall, as she made her escape. On guard for her lady's maid and the butler, Henrietta tiptoed across the landing and down the grand staircase. In the foyer, she halted, glanced left and then right, continued to the morning room, and paused at the terrace doors.

The moon cast a silvery glow on the flagged stones, and a soft breeze thrummed through her hair, as she ventured outside and down the pebbled path. At the back gate, she lifted the latch and skulked into the alley, where she rushed to the mews.

To her surprise, a soft yellow light emanated from the window of the small quarters in which her father lived, while the family resided in town, and she considered it a sign that fate smiled upon her. She rapped her knuckles on the oak panel, and she started when her father snatched open the door.

"Henrietta?" Shock invested his features, as he blinked. "What are you doing here, at this late hour?"

"I need to speak with you, and it is urgent." Now the pain she had kept at bay burst forth, as the incoming tide, and she wept without restraint. "Please, Papa, I beg you. I must leave, now." Pushing him aside, she rushed into the modest chamber. "Indeed, I must away, before Ernest finds out—"

"Before Ernest finds out—what, my little bird?"

The floor seemed to pitch and roll beneath her feet, and the room spun out of control, as she told herself she must have been suffering from some strange delirium. She had to have imagined Ernest's entreaty. Slowly. Painfully slowly, she rotated and faced her doom.

"What are you doing here?" Praying for calm, she pretended nothing was wrong. That her heart was not breaking into countless tiny pieces. "Why are you here?"

"I could ask the same of you." He narrowed his stare and then arched a brow. "Going somewhere?"

"I thought to spare you the difficulties of a broken promise." Shivering, she fought to maintain control, even as her knees buckled, and he lurched forward to catch her.

"Henrietta, you make no sense, but that is not your fault, as you had a terrible fright, tonight." Expecting criticism and recriminations, she was stunned when he pressed his lips to her forehead. "Darling, sit down, as you are still pale, and I am worried about you."

"Do you not want me to leave?" She struggled and dropped her bundles. "Are you not preparing to send me away?"

"What on earth ever gave you such a ridiculous notion?" Wrapping an arm about her waist, he pulled her close. "Sweetheart, you are not thinking clearly."

"Yes, I am." Stock-still, she thrust her chin. "You were not with me, when I woke, and you are always with me. You promised I would never pass a night not spent in your embrace, and you were not there. I was alone."

In that moment, Barrington cleared his throat. "Er—Graham, what say we step outside, and let my brother smooth things with Henrietta?"

"That is an excellent suggestion, my lord." Papa scowled. "Because I might be moved to violence, if I hear more. As it is, I believe I must insist Lord Ernest marry my daughter."

"Sir, trust me, that was never in doubt." Ernest cupped her cheek, angled his head, and bestowed upon her a thorough kiss, which left her swimming in a sea of confusion. "Now, you will sit."

With that, he plopped into a chair and tugged her into his lap.

"Why were you not there?" Random memories flitted through her brain, and she tried but failed to apprehend their meaning. "What happened after we departed the Hogart's?"

"It was quiet in the coach, because you were so pale, and we worried for your health." He nuzzled her temple. "You could not stop shaking, and before we arrived home, you fainted. So I carried you to your bed, left orders that you were not to be disturbed, because I planned to tend you, myself, and I joined my brother and your father, to strategize our next move."

Unable to withstand any more uncertainty, Henrietta burst into tears. "My lord, I am so sorry I shamed you in front of your friends."

"But you did nothing of the sort." Drawing his handkerchief from his coat pocket, he frowned and then dried her cheeks. "Indeed, you were glorious, as you put that dreadful Bland woman in her place, and set Agnes Dudley on her heels. Daresay half the people in the room were cheering for you."

"So you are not angry with me?" Hope glimmered, yet she was afraid to trust it. "You will not send me away?"

"Never." Cradling her head, he swayed from side to side. "I am going to marry the stablemaster's daughter, and I do not give a damn what anyone thinks."

"I should have been honest with you." She sniffed. "More important, I should have been honest with myself, but I did so wish to please you. Yet, I suspect I will never be anything more than I am right now."

"Henrietta, you have never done anything less, and I owe you an apology. Indulge me." Resting his chin to her crown, he sighed, and she felt it all the way to her toes. "Do you recall the summer parties my parents used to hold, every August, when you often loomed in the shrubbery and peered through the back parlor window, pressing your nose to the glass?"

"I do." Safe and warm in his hold, she let go the tension that tied her gut in knots and relaxed.

"And how I stole various sweetmeats, which I took to you?" When she nodded, he chuckled. "We used to sit beneath the old yew, on Oker Hill, throw our own private celebration, and stuff our bellies full, until that year my father caught you staring at his guests."

"I was six, and Lord Ravenwood insisted my father punish me." That Henrietta would never forget. "In fact, he ordered my father to spank me, on pain of termination, and Lord Ravenwood refused to leave until it was done, thus he sat and watched my humiliation. It was the only time my father ever struck me, and he wept with me, afterward."

"How I hated my father for that." Ernest tightened his grip. "Though we were but children, I vowed, then and there, that you would one day stand at my side, for all to see, as my wife. That you would dine at our table. You would sleep in the master suite. You would wear the finest clothes. You would boast glittering gems. You would dance at the balls. You would want for nothing, and it is an oath I intend to keep, as a man."

"But I only want you," she replied, in a small voice.

"Ah, Hen, you slay me." Grasping the hair at her nape, he tipped back her head and claimed her mouth in a searing kiss that curled her toes. After several heated, desperately tender minutes, he retreated, only to hug her close. "My mistake was in trying to remake you, but that ended, this evening. Yet all is not lost, and Barrington set in motion a scheme that should settle the matter."

"Oh?" She was not sure what to make of that revelation. "Does it involve another musicale at the Hogart's?"

"No." He laughed. "But we can discuss it, in the morning." In a flash, he rose and carried her with him. "Right now, I want to return to your room, get out of these clothes, and make love."

"That is an idea I can wholeheartedly support." With her nose, she traced the curve of his ear. "Ernest, I do love you."

"And I love you, my little bird." Then he snickered, as he swept her outside. "Gentlemen, crisis averted, as Henrietta bestows her heart upon this beggar."

"That is a relief." Papa glanced at her and smiled. "You need to rest, as Lord Ernest told me what happened, but Lord Ravenwood will make everything right, and he insists you do him a great favor."

"Really?" Perplexed by the cryptic comment, she canted her head. "How so?"

"Indeed, this is a chance at redemption, for me. It is an opportunity for me to take care of my little brother, for a change, so I thank you, Henrietta." Rocking on his heels, Barrington grinned. "As for my plan, given I am a marquess, that counts for something. But suffice it to say, I have friends in high places."

CHAPTER TWELVE

The following evening, at the prescribed hour, Ernest and Henrietta, with Barrington acting as chaperone, descended the Ravenwood brougham, at Hyde Park, to partake of the Promenade. Coiffed to perfection, his fiancée cut a flawless picture of the perfect English noblewoman, yet one of her unique creations set her apart from the crowd. Now, if only she would stop fidgeting.

"Are you sure about this?" She bit her lip and surveyed the throng. "Can we not come back next year? Or, perhaps, in the following century, when they are all dead?"

"Do not fear, my little bird, as I am with you." With Hen firmly anchored on his arm, he led her into the rotation. Yet he ignored the not so polite stares and the number of those who gave them their backs. Were they so perfect? Bloody hypocrites. "And I shall not leave your side."

"I fear I am going vomit." Pale, she slowed and inhaled a deep breath. "Whatever happens, do not let me faint in front of the *ton*."

"Darling, relax." Was it too soon? Had he overestimated her fortitude? "I promise, everything will be fine. And you will not vomit, because you have had naught but dry toast and weak tea, this morning. I told you to take lunch, but you refused. Daresay, it is the effects of ravenous hunger that plague you."

"But I am too nervous to eat." With her hand, she clutched her throat and toyed with the diamond necklace he insisted she wear. "What if Mrs. Dudley or her horrible sister is here? What if I am confronted?"

"I wager you can handle them." Barrington positioned himself alongside Henrietta, sandwiching her between two estimable Howes. "By the by, I am sorry Florence is not here, but I forbade her from attending, because she is not rested after last night. She was so furious, I feared she might be moved to violence, if she spied either of the two harridans, here, and I would rather not have my pregnant wife arrested for assault."

"I understand, completely." Henrietta glanced from left to right, and Ernest noted the lines of strain etched about her eyes. All of a sudden, she started. "Oh, dear."

"What is wrong?" It was then he discovered the source of her discomfit, a rapidly approaching Beryl Hogart, accompanied by Lady Jersey, and he whispered, "Easy, as she is the soul of charity."

"Lord Ravenwood, Lord Ernest, and Miss Graham, it is so good to see you." Profuse with dramatic emotion, Mrs. Hogart made a show of addressing Henrietta. "I had it on my list to pay call, but you so generously grant me an audience, instead, and I am honor-bound to make my apologies for the shameful treatment meted on you, while you were guests in my home." With a lace-edged handkerchief, she daubed her large nose and sniffed. "I only hope you can find it in your heart to forgive me for the egregious breach in decorum, Miss Graham. I can assure you, such behavior is not the norm at my events. And I said to Mrs. Dudley and Ms. Bland, 'Never again will you darken my doorstep or partake of my musicales.'"

"To be denied such joy is a very great tragedy, indeed, and they are all the poorer for it, but you mistake the situation, Mrs. Hogart." As Ernest anticipated, his bride-to-be displayed her characteristic humility, while he swallowed a snort and Barrington covered his mouth. "I am as much to blame as anyone, and I am so sorry I ruined your daughters' wonderful performance."

"Oh, you are a woman of discriminating taste and uncommon judgment." With a cat-that-ate-the-canary smirk, Mrs. Hogart regarded Lady Jersey. "Did I not tell you the very same?" Then she gazed at Ernest. "And I said as much, last night, did I not, Lord Ernest?"

To wit he nodded.

"So you did, Beryl." Lady Jersey inclined her head. "We have not been properly introduced, but I am Lady Jersey, and I must compliment you on your fashions, Miss Graham, as they really are quite remarkable."

"Thank you, my lady." As Florence instructed, Henrietta curtseyed.

"Miss Graham, you would do me a very great honor, if you would consent to create something for my Miranda, for the Duke of Rylan's ball, because we shall announce her wedding, in *The Times*, just prior to the gala."

Now that was something Ernest had not predicted, but it played right into his plans, as Mrs. Hogart pressed a fist to her chest. "I beg you, do not refuse me, and I shall pledge unlimited entry to my musicales."

"*Oh.*" Henrietta responded with a timid smile. That threat, alone, was enough to send Ernest running for Derbyshire, but he persevered for his future wife. "I am overwhelmed by your kindness, and the honor is mine, Mrs. Hogart. If you bring your daughter to Howe House, I will take her measurements, and we can discuss colors and materials, as well as her vision and style, because it is important to capture the wearer's personality to achieve a perfect fit."

"Did you hear that, Lady Jersey?" Mrs. Hogart gloated. "Just wait till I tell Mrs. Ponsonby my daughter is getting a Graham original." Then she waved. "Well, enjoy the Promenade. Cheerio."

The surrounding pedestrians whispered and pointed, and Ernest gave Henrietta a gentle nudge. "Let us continue, sweetheart."

"What just happened?" She rubbed the back of her neck. "And why is everyone staring?"

"Because you just got the official approval of not one but two of the most influential matriarchs in the *ton*," Barrington explained.

"Indeed, Beryl Hogart and Lady Jersey wield considerable power in the social arena, and no one will gainsay them, for fear of retribution and censure." Ernest spied his conspirators, who gathered in their usual place, and steered her in their direction. "But Mrs. Hogart is also one of the most obliging figures in London."

"That is why everyone attends her loathsome musicales." Henrietta nodded to a passing couple, which acknowledged her, and Ernest sighed in relief. "And if I do an adequate job of designing for Miranda—"

"You are ensured a lifetime of sore ears, as well as Mrs. Hogart's good opinion." Barrington snickered. "Given the ensemble is to accompany a wedding announcement, I wager the matchmaking mamas will beat a path to your door."

"But I am one person." Another group of ladies dipped their chins in unison, and Henrietta responded, in kind. "I cannot possibly serve everyone. Will that not hurt me, in their estimation?"

"Perhaps, we should look into purchasing a boutique, of your very own, if that would make you happy." Ernest began running the numbers, as he enjoyed finance. "You could interview and hire additional seamstresses, to help sew your exclusive designs."

"My lord, I must confess the idea thrills me, but I have very high standards." She bit her lip, and he could almost read her thoughts. "Still, if I require samples of their work, and I speak with each prospective candidate, we just might succeed in building a profitable enterprise."

"Ah, I love it when you talk money." Thus they arrived at the pivotal moment, and Ernest winked at his allies.

"Ravenwood and Lord Ernest." His Grace, Blake Elliott, the Duke of Rylan squared his shoulders, and it was as though all of society held their collective breath. "And this must be the inimitable Miss Graham, I presume? The Duke of Rylan, at your service." Then he broke character and cast a devilish countenance. "My duchess speaks of little else besides your designs, and I wonder if I might impinge upon you to make a dress for her?"

"Well, now you have done it." On cue, His Grace, Damian Seymour, the Duke of Weston elbowed Rylan, and the ducal duo, well known for their longstanding affiliation, launched their scheme. "If you buy a gown for Lenore, then I must purchase one for

Lucilla."

"And that is my problem, how?" Rylan scoffed. "It is not as if you cannot afford it, cheap bastard." To Henrietta, he said, "Spare no expense, Miss Graham, as I would have only the finest for my duchess."

"I swear, you are intent on bankrupting my dukedom." Weston shoved aside the other duke. "I shall pay double for a garment of equal quality."

"My card, Miss Graham." Rylan extended a hand.

"And mine." Weston pushed to the fore.

"Your Graces, there is no need to argue, as I shall be delighted to outfit both duchesses." For the first time since they arrived in the park, Henrietta surrendered Ernest's escort, collected the cards, and stashed them in her reticule.

And then a veritable sea of ladies, demanding similar services, swamped her.

"I told you, the *ton* is naught but a polished mob." Barrington clucked his tongue, as they removed to a safe place to watch the theatrics. "They love a scandal, second only to a love story, which you have given them."

"She is going to need a large storefront." Ernest made a mental note to contact his solicitor, at once. In that instant, Hen caught his gaze, and the sheer elation he glimpsed well nigh brought him to tears. "Thank you, for doing this."

"I should thank you, brother." Barrington patted Ernest on the back. "While this may sound sentimental, I mean every word. You made me the man I am today, and I am grateful for the opportunity to repay you. So, now that we have made a triumph of the situation, what is next for you and Henrietta?"

"That is easy." Hope glimmered and unfurled, filling his chest with unparalleled anticipation for a bright future. "After the wedding, I would start a family."

"I thought you commenced that, back at Garring." Barrington snorted. "Given the ruckus. Good God, she has incited a riot."

"We did, yet she shows no sign of progress, much to my disappointment." Five more ladies joined the throng, and Ernest basked in pride as Henrietta managed the commotion. "But we are still finding our way."

"Well, you will forgive me if I say you are on your own with that particular task." Barrington shifted his weight. "It is all I can do to keep pace with Florence, not that I am complaining."

"Brother, I am happy to submit I get your meaning, and the work is good." Between every new address, his little bird met his stare, investing each brief connection with a singular phrase he could not mistake, *I love you*, and he could not wait to get her home and enact a private celebration. "And believe me, I require no help in that respect."

~

From a cloudless sky, sunlight filtered through the stained glass windows, projecting a colorful mosaic on the wooden floor of the nave at St. George's Hanover Square. An array of nobles, garbed in their best attire, filled the box pews, as Ernest, immaculate in a coat of Bath superfine, turned to Henrietta and pledged, "My heart will be your shelter, and my arms will be your home."

Of course, his warm and reassuring embrace had been her haven since they consummated their love, at Garring Manor, and she passed each night enveloped by his strong body. Through tears of joy, she made the same vow, and in a flurry of activity that left her giddy, she raced down the aisle with her new husband.

At the curb, the Ravenwood landau awaited, and he lifted her into the squabs before joining her.

"Upon my word, we are married." She gazed at him and blinked. "Or is this a much-cherished dream? If so, woe to the person who wakes me."

"My darling wife, and how I have longed to address you as such, for good or ill, we are bound for all eternity, and no one can take you from me, again." Onlookers shouted for them to kiss, and Ernest glanced at her and smiled. "Shall we oblige them?"

She nodded with enthusiasm. "Yes, please."

Chuckling, he set his mouth to hers, ever so briefly, and the crowd cheered.

"*Oy.*" He called to the coachman. "Drive on."

"What is the rush?" Enjoying the moment, she spied Barrington, Florence, and her father, and waved. "Oh, this is such fun."

"I have a surprise for you, and we are due at Howe House, for our wedding breakfast." Twining his fingers in hers, he pressed his lips to her gloved knuckles. "And I would have thought you famished, by now, given I exercised you quite thoroughly this morning."

"If memory serves, I did my share of nibbling, much to your expressed pleasure." And her cheeks burned as she recalled their naughty habits, but never did she suffer shame, because he was her man. "In fairness, I only did what you taught me."

"And you did well, my dear, as I want you, even now." Flushing red, he claimed another sweet kiss, just as the rig pulled to the curb. "Ah, we are here."

"What are we doing on Bond Street?" Curious, she glanced left and then right. "Are we meeting someone?"

"No, my love." With an air of smug satisfaction, he motioned to an empty building. "My gift to you, on our most special day." He pointed for emphasis. "It has four floors, as well as a storage area, below stairs, and ample room for expansion. If necessary, I can purchase the shop, next door."

"You cannot be serious." Studying the red brick structure, trimmed in Portland stone, she noted a curious sign above the massive windows. "Ernest, it is too much."

"But we talked about it, and we agreed you should open your own boutique." As usual, he leaped in headfirst with nary a care for the specifics. "Since we journey to the Continent, in a fortnight, I thought we could buy fabrics and notions on our trip to Paris. That would give you the opportunity to examine the fashions and incorporate more ideas into your designs. Would you not like that?"

"You warned me we would not see much beyond the confines of our suite." She giggled. "Do you renege, my cherished husband? Because I rather look forward to being ravished."

"I love it when you call me that, and I am going to bury my face between your luscious thighs, tonight." At his bold pronouncement, which she doubted not for an instant, she tensed. "Now, do you not like it? Am I not to be rewarded for my thoughtfulness and generosity?"

"I adore it and you." Then she leaned close and whispered her intentions, as she planned to thank him when they adjourned to his chamber, and he groaned. "Think about that, as we partake of our breakfast."

"Trust me, I shall be hard pressed to forget it, as I may be erect until the New Year." He shifted his weight. "And I should keep my coat buttoned, lest I embarrass myself at our party."

"Then, by all means, let us away." Then she tapped her chin. "Only, I would know what the sign says. I suppose that is French, but I do not know what it means. Is it the name of the last business that occupied the space?"

"Ah, that is my touch, and I would ask you not to change it, as I suspect you will appreciate the significance." Wrapping an arm about her shoulders, he nuzzled her temple. "*Le Petite Oiseau* is French for 'the little bird.'"

"Oh, Ernest, I *love* it." For the umpteenth time that day, she wrestled with happy tears and fumbled for her handkerchief. "I still cannot believe everything worked out for us, and we are finally united."

"I know, sweetheart." He cupped her cheek. "Regardless of the past and those who conspired against us, we triumphed, and now I would celebrate our future."

Despite the open-air landau, Ernest bent his head and kissed her. And kept kissing her.

A few minutes later, the ceremonial equipage came to a halt before Howe House, and they descended to the graveled drive. Before she could take a step, he bent and swept her off her feet.

Laughing, he charged into the foyer, where Barrington and Florence lingered.

"How did it go?" Barrington asked. "Did she like it?"

"She loved it." Ernest set her down and slipped an arm about her waist. To Henrietta, he said, "My brother located the vacant shop, and I suspect we may need to secure the building alongside, because my wife is brilliant, and I predict she will be a smashing success."

"If the requests we have fielded are any indication, you are right." Florence gave Henrietta a quick peck on the cheek. "My dear, your unconventional wedding gown has caused an even bigger stir than your ceremony, and the ballroom is abuzz with ladies just waiting to place an order."

"Really?" Henrietta snorted in astonishment. "I did not anticipate that, because my implication was quite elementary."

"And I am interested to know the meaning behind the frock." Ernest retreated and scrutinized her from top to toe. "While you are stunning in whatever you wear, I had thought you might employ all the colors of the rainbow, as well as your signature, hand-painted flowers."

"Yet hers was a genius maneuver." Florence shook her head. "Bedecked in all white, she stood out from the crowd. Indeed, we could not miss her, as she walked the aisle on Graham's arm."

"Yet, even that was not my intent." Henrietta smoothed her skirts and adjusted a sleeve. "Rather, I look upon my garb as a chance to start anew, and the pristine white, with minimal ornamentation and lace in the same hue, symbolizes a blank canvas, of a sort. It is my declaration, as I begin my life as part of something greater than myself, and I would leave behind the ugliness of the past, when I venture forth as a lady."

"Darling, I am touched beyond words by your considerate nature." Ernest furrowed his brow. "But I am proud of you, just as you are."

"Thank you." She brushed a lock of blond hair from his forehead. "And I am equally proud of my husband."

"Then let us join our guests, before you two combust." Barrington snickered. "There will be plenty of time for that, later."

"You are one to talk." Ernest elbowed his elder brother. "If I recall, you locked Florence in your private apartment for three days after your nuptials, and the noises—"

"That is quite enough." Florence rolled her eyes and steered Barrington toward the hall. "Now, let us adjourn to the ballroom."

Despite the complimentary mentions in the gossip columns, leading up to the big event, Henrietta struggled with doubts about her reception. While Florence explained there would always be those who would not receive a servant's daughter, society could be fickle, and the weak could be swayed by the powerful people firmly entrenched in Henrietta's corner.

One such person was the first to greet her, as she entered the expansive, grand dining room, which boasted Egyptian décor by Thomas Hope.

"Percy." When she shouted his name, he splayed his palms in welcome, and she hugged him. "Oh, now we are related, treasured cousin."

"Yes, we are, dear Mrs. Howe." Even as he grinned, a hint of sadness colored his blue eyes. "Aw, I wish you the best, old friend. Perhaps, someday, you will help me find true love and redemption, because I am lonely, Henrietta."

"I will, Percy." Perched on tiptoes, she kissed his cheek. "I promise, I will. And you must visit Ernest and I, at Whitstone, because you are never alone. You are family, and I expect you to celebrate the holidays with us."

"Thank you, sweet lady." With that, he bowed.

The next friendly face brought her to a quick halt, and she curtseyed, as Ernest bowed. "Your Grace, I am so honored you could attend my special day."

"Posh." The Duchess of Rylan waved, dismissively. "I would not miss it for the world, and I wore the gown you sewed, especially, to show my support."

"I am so glad it meets with Your Grace's approval." Just then, Henrietta caught sight of the Duchess of Weston. "And I am doubly blessed, as I see Her Grace sports hers, as well."

"Indeed, my sister is thrilled with your creation, as it suits her." The duchess admired her sister's attire. "Your design to accommodate her missing appendage is nothing short of remarkable, and we are grateful. But I wanted to have a brief word with you, about a personal matter, if I may."

"Of course." Henrietta glanced at Ernest. "My lord, I will meet you at our table, and I will not be long."

"That is fine, darling." He kissed her hand. "As I need to arrange a toast."

"So, how may I be of service, Your Grace?" Curious, Henrietta moved to stand near a wall. "What can I do for you?"

"Actually, it is what I can do for you that I would discuss." The duchess lowered her voice. "You see, you and I have much in common, given you are not the first unconventional bride, and I wager you will not be the last, as I was not to the manor born. Indeed, I am but a general's daughter, as is my sister. I met that insufferable man I call a husband, when he almost ran me aground with his horse, and we fell in love aboard his ship, but he led me to believe he was but a sea captain in service to His Majesty. Scoundrel that he was, Blake never told me the truth of his rank, until after we docked in London, and he owned my heart. Like you, I thought I was not good enough to wed a duke, but he proved me wrong, and I found my place in society, just as you will find yours." She took Hen's hand and squeezed her fingers. "There will be times when you doubt yourself, when you wonder if everyone considers you a failure and predicts your fall, and you will want to flee. Mark my words, and heed my advice. Walk, never run from the *ton*, and never let them see you cry, as they admire strength and seize upon the slightest hint of trepidation to turn and rend you. As my husband so correctly asserted, love knows no rank or social etiquette. All that matters is that Lord Ernest chose you, and you accepted him."

"Thank you, Your Grace." Again moved to happy tears, Henrietta sniffed. "You know not what your support means to me."

"Oh, I think I do." Her Grace stepped to the rear and nodded. "Now, I believe it past due for you to join your husband, as he stares at you, and this is your time to shine."

"If you will excuse me, Your Grace." Buoyant with renewed confidence, Henrietta curtseyed and all but skipped to the table of honor, where Ernest waited.

"Is everything all right?" He pulled her close. "What did the Duchess want?"

"Everything is wonderful." His boyish countenance, bereft of the worries that plagued their courtship, melted her heart, and she eased to the chair he held for her. "And she imparted sage wisdom." Toying with the crystal stem of her glass, she prepared for the feast, when she noted he remained on guard.

"If I may have your attention." Calm fell upon the massive room, as Ernest loomed tall. "I know it is not the usual custom for the groom to begin the festivities, but since my marriage has been anything but customary, and my love affair with my bride defies the norm, I hope you will grant me a bit of license, in this respect." In that instant, she held her breath, and he gazed at her and winked. "You see, I have known Henrietta from the morning she entered this world, and from that moment, she has been my lady. Although we were separated for a while, she remained a guiding light during my darkest hours, such that I cannot recall a time when I was not hers, and I am convinced she was fated to be mine. So I ask everyone to join me, as I toast my incomparable bride. My Henrietta. My stablemaster's daughter."

EPILOGUE

September, 1819

The sun danced on the horizon on an unusually warm evening, as Ernest stood on the entrance steps of Whitstone and waved farewell to Barrington. In the months since Ernest married Henrietta, the builders completed the renovations to the palatial estate, and his bride put her own decorative touches on the place, when they retired to their summerhouse, which made it truly their home. As he studied the elegant décor, he reflected on his life, and he realized he had everything he ever wanted.

He was closer than ever to his brother, he wed the woman of his dreams, and they purchased a home near Garring Manor. And every night, he endeavored to produce a member of the next generation of Howes, although his labors proved fruitless. The work was good, so he was not complaining.

"Did Barrington depart?" Ah, his charming wife glided into the foyer. Just looking at her made him want to cry. "Did you remember to send the silk shawl I made for Florence?"

"Yes, my brother is en route to Garring, and he has the package you so graciously wrapped." From his coat pocket, he drew an envelope. "By the by, a missive was delivered for you, and I intercepted the messenger at the front gate, as I returned from the race."

"Did you best Barrington?" With a feminine smile, she approached, slipped her arms about his waist, and inclined her head to receive his kiss on her cheek. "Or are you going to pout all evening, as you did after your last contest? I warn you, I will not tolerate your sulking about, when I have arranged a lovely dinner in our sitting room."

"But I thought you could not resist my pout, and you compensated so admirably for my disappointment." In play, he ravished the swanlike curve of her neck and savored her answering giggle. "And if memory serves, you labored into the wee hours of the morning. Given I won today's challenge, what say we celebrate with a repeat performance?"

"Food, first, as I am famished." As if to impress upon him her point, her belly grumbled in protest, and he laughed.

"All right, my little bird." In play, he swatted her bottom, and they ascended the stairs. "What news from London?"

"Not good, I suspect." She tore into the envelope, unfolded the stationary, and hummed. "Just as I feared, we are swamped with new orders for the impending Season, and Mr. Fairley wants to hire six additional seamstresses." When he opened the door to their shared private apartment, she strolled inside and huffed. "More than twenty bolts of silk were ruined by the leak in the roof, and Mrs. Hogart has commissioned an entire wardrobe for herself and for Margaret, because she is convinced one of my gowns will land her daughter a husband."

"I submit it will take more than one of your fabulous creations to snare some poor, unsuspecting fool to marry into that family, and there is only one Archibald Kleinfeld." In the sitting room, he noted the small table for two, set near the windows, and the candles. So, he was to be seduced. "Although she possesses a tidy fortune, and that is enough to entice several prospective candidates."

"Actually, Margaret is quite lovely, in her own way." From her escritoire, Henrietta collected her inkwell, pen, and paper. Then she took her seat, which he held for her. "What she requires is a unique collection to emphasize her assets."

"And a new music tutor." He snorted with laughter.

"Now, now." As she sketched, a familiar habit, she furrowed her brow, and Ernest assumed his place just to her right, because she preferred to keep him within reach, and that was fine with him. "Do not be rude, because I think Margaret is sorely underestimated by the *ton*, and I would lend my aid to her cause."

"You have become quite the society lady, my fetching bride." Indeed, she was in demand, yet she remained the same sweet-tempered girl he adored. "Are you planning to venture into the marriage mart business?"

"Not a chance." She cast a side-glance. "You may commence the service, as I just want to note a few ideas before I forget them."

"All right." He drew the napkin from his plate and discovered a small bundle. "What is this?"

Henrietta merely shrugged.

With care, he unfolded the brown paper, studied the item, reflected on the significance—and froze.

"I am thinking of producing a new line of clothing." When he gaped at her, she shimmered with unmasked joy. "Do you believe I shall find equal success with children's garb?"

For a few seconds, Ernest struggled to respond, because he feared he might make a cake of himself. "Does this mean what I pray it means?"

"Yes." She nodded once.

"Darling." In a flash, he pushed from the table and knelt beside her. "How do you feel? Are you well? Are you tired? Should I summon the doctor?"

"Ernest, calm yourself." She giggled and kissed him. "I am beside myself, and we feel fine, but you are white as a sheet."

"I am worried about you." Lifting her in his arms, he glanced left and then right. He strolled into their inner chamber, paused at the foot of their four-poster, frowned, and then returned to the sitting room. "Bloody hell, I am going to be a father."

"My love, I beg you, put me down before you drop me, because you appear on the verge of swooning." At last, he returned to his chair and settled her safely in his lap, and she wound her arms about his neck. "Shall I fetch you a brandy, because you look like you could use a drink."

"No." He tightened his hold. "Do not leave me, as I need to hold you."

It dawned on him then that he held his wife *and* their babe in his grasp, and he bent his head and wept without shame.

"Ernest, my sweet husband, do not cry." As usual, she knew just how to appeal to him, as she bestowed upon him a series of flirty kisses along the crest of his ear, continuing along the curve of his jaw. "You are going to make a wonderful father, and we are going to do this together."

"As we have done everything, my little bird." Twining his fingers in hers, he brought her bare knuckles to his lips and then pressed her open palm to his cheek. "Do you know that I wake, every day, and search for you? That there is still a tiny bit of doubt that this is our life?"

"Yes, because I do it, too." She rested her forehead to his. "But it gets easier, with each passing morning, when I wake to you, and you hold me in your arms. And at night, when I fall asleep in your unyielding embrace,

I know you are here. I only wish I could find a way to prevent the nightmares of your father's abuse that still plague you, because your torment breaks my heart."

"But you compensate admirably." He gave her a gentle squeeze, as so many possibilities sprang to life. "And I am so excited about your news. If it is a girl, I am going to spoil her. Of course, you will dress her. And it if it is a boy, I am going to mentor him, and teach him all he needs to know to survive, but I will never hurt him."

"You will do your best, and that is all anyone can ask." She rubbed her nose to his. "Do you know what I want to do?"

"What, sweetheart?" No matter the request, he would give her anything. "Tell me what you want."

"Do you remember how we used to sit on the floor, behind the sofa, in the back parlor, and eat the extra scones and strawberry preserves left from your mother's afternoon teas?" When he nodded, she grinned and gazed at the table. "What say we dine on the carpet, as we did then? Only now we have no fear of discovery or retribution, and we can linger as we choose."

"I love that idea." He lifted her from his lap.

Working in concert, they resituated the meal, with place settings arranged in a less than elegant yet comfy presentation. She kicked off her slippers, and he doffed his boots and coat. As he collected a couple of large, fluffy pillows, she poured the wine. With their feast spread before them, he supported her, as she knelt and eased to the cushion, and he squatted beside her.

"It seems like yesterday, does it not?" She inclined her head and opened her mouth, as he fed her a juicy morsel of roasted chicken. "And you are still taking care of me."

"That is my chief priority." Footsteps in the hall caught his attention, and he halted, mid-chew, as a shudder of alarm traipsed his spine, and stared at Henrietta, as she mirrored his stance. For a brief instant, tension weighed heavy, until all fell quiet.

In unison, they blinked.

Then they burst into laughter.

"Old habits really are hard to break." She daubed the corner of her mouth with a napkin, and he relaxed. "For a minute, I sought a hiding place."

"As did I." He chuckled and then sobered, as he surveyed their suite, bedecked in an odd array of their combined personal effects, indicative of their mutual existence. Indeed, they were two like souls, so perfectly matched as to render the distinctions between them invisible, despite everything they endured. Not even an eleven-year separation could divide them. "But there will be no more running for us, because we are as one, and the future is ours."

ABOUT BARBARA DEVLIN

USA Today Bestselling Author Barbara Devlin was born a storyteller, but it was a weeklong vacation to Bethany Beach, DE that forever changed her life. The little house her parents rented had a collection of books by Kathleen Woodiwiss, which exposed Barbara to the world of romance, and Shanna remains a personal favorite. Barbara writes heartfelt historical romances that feature flawed heroes who may know how to seduce a woman but know nothing of marriage. And she prefers feisty but smart heroines who sometimes save the hero, before they find their happily ever after. Barbara earned an MA in English and continued a course of study for a Doctorate in Literature and Rhetoric. She happily considered herself an exceedingly eccentric English professor, until success in Indie publishing lured her into writing, full-time, featuring her fictional knighthood, the Brethren of the Coast.

Connect with Barbara Devlin at BarbaraDevlin.com, where you can sign up for her newsletter, The Knightly News.
Facebook:
https://www.facebook.com/BarbaraDevlinAuthor
Twitter: @barbara_devlin

KATHRYN LE VEQUE'S KINDLE WORLD OF DE WOLFE PACK
Lone Wolfe
The Big Bad De Wolfe
Tall, Dark & De Wolfe (January 2018)

OTHER STORIES
Magick, Straight Up
The Stablemaster's Daughter

Made in the USA
Middletown, DE
13 May 2019